A Mirror of Miracles

Naomi Sharp

DEDICATION

I dedicate this book to Elizabeth and Carol. Our coincidental meeting and many years of friendship, as we travel along this road called life together with laughter, love and light.

CONTENTS

1 TWO DESTINIES INTERTWINING

'I'll go and get the duvet, mom!' Hugh yelled from the top of the stairs as he disappeared into the spare bedroom. They all began to set up the living room for another movie night. Ally sat on the couch staring intently at her computer as her fingers tapped on the keys. Ben crouched by the open fire as he struck a match and watched for a moment as the wood burst into flames and illuminated the room with a glow of love. He stood up and turned round, sinking his hands deep into his jeans pockets. He looked at Ally and watched the multiple expressions Ally was making: happiness, shock, sadness, confusion. 'That's some conversation you're having there' Ben said with a cheeky smile. He made his way across to the couch and sat down by her side. Draping his arm across the back of the couch, he leaned over to look at the computer screen.

As he began to skim the words it wasn't long until he got the idea of what the email was about. As his eyes reached the bottom he saw 'Love always, Molly and Co'. Ben glanced up with a look of confusion on his face, 'Who's Molly?' he asked curiously. Ally continued tapping away on the keys, the sound becoming more frantic. 'Earth to Ally!' Ben said a bit louder. Then a thud echoed around the room. They both shot a look behind them and saw Hugh sprawled out on the floor on top of the duvet. Hugh spun over and pretending to wrestle with the duvet. 'I got me a wild one!' he said, like John Wayne, as he became even more tangled up in the duvet.

Ally looked blankly across the room and then turned back around and continued to type. 'Don't worry, I'll help' Ben said sarcastically as he stood up and began to make his way across to where Hugh was trying to scoop up the duvet. He was struggling as each time he got another armful, more duvet fell to the ground. Ally nodded, not taking any notice as she became engrossed in the conversation once again. Ben scooped up the duvet under one arm and then scooped up Hugh under the other. 'Maybe you'll be able to tell me Hugh. Who is Molly and Co?' he said, placing Hugh on the sofa. 'Oh, they're some of our friends back in England. Molly is the same age as me. Mom met Molly's mum when we were really small. I used to stay at Molly's house if mom needed some time to herself and Molly used to stay at mine. There was one time that we went and had a sleep over at her Nana's house, Nana O was her name but I never saw her again.'

'How come you guys haven't mentioned them before?' Ben asked as he sat down next to Ally. Hugh re-positioned himself, laying across both of them. Ally interrupted as she punched with her finger on the enter button and there was a whoosh sound as the email was sent. Ally closed the lid on her laptop and looked across to Ben. 'I did hear you the first time, I just had to finish that before I answered' Ally said. Before she could continue further, Ally was drowned out by Hugh's voice. 'Shhh!!!' he hissed as they heard the drum roll of the opening credits of the movie.

Ally mimed 'I'll tell you later' towards Ben. Ben looked back, not convinced everything was alright but made an OK sign with his fingers and gave her one of his charming smiles. Ally let her head rest on his shoulder as they all sat and became engrossed in the movie.

As the movie progressed, Ben watched the flames of the fire start to die back and the room be lit up from the glow of the embers. He felt the weight on his shoulder get heavier as he glanced across to see Ally fast asleep. He reached forward to the remote control and turned the volume down a couple of clicks as Hugh serenaded the final credits of the movie with his snoring. 'One movie night we are going to make it through without anyone falling asleep' Ben chuckled to himself.

Ben carefully began to shuffle as he lifted Ally's head and placed it down on the couch, trying not to wake her. He scooped up a limp Hugh, who could sleep through a hurricane, and carried him across the living room. As Ben began to walk up the stairs he stopped halfway, taking in a gasp of air. 'Either Hugh is getting heavier or Ally's keeping me too well' Ben thought as he took the next step up, his legs getting heavier and heavier.

'Come on Ben, you can rope cattle, win championships, you can make these last two steps' he continued, giving himself a pep talk 'One step, two steps'. As he reached the top he let out a large sigh of relief. 'I think I need to rekindle my relationship with the gym' Ben said, shaking his head as he looked back down what now looked like a very trivial achievement. Hugh started to wriggle in his arms, 'Hang on little man' Ben said as he swiftly walked across to Hugh's bedroom, trying to reach his bed before he woke up. Hugh snuggled his head into the crook of Ben's neck and became still once more.

Ben stopped, savouring the moment. 'What if I hadn't had gone to that country fair and rodeo? What if I hadn't gone to the bar and kissed Ally? I would have missed out on all this' he thought to himself. He squeezed Hugh at the thought. 'Someone is definitely watching over me and blessing me to have you' he whispered as he lowered Hugh into his bed and pulled the duvet up to cover him.

Ben leaned over and kissed Hugh on the forehead. 'Goodnight, Champion' he whispered. As he looked up he glanced at Hugh's new vision wall he had been creating that day. He looked at all the different pictures of people he wanted to meet, places he wanted to go and experiences he wanted to have. As he smiled to himself he turned around and began to walk across the bedroom back to the landing. He did a hopscotch motion as he dodged the floor boards that creaked. He pulled the door, just leaving a slither of light.

Ben skipped down the stairs, ready to scoop up and carry the next love in his life. As he reached the last step he stopped abruptly and looked across the living room to see an empty couch and the fire put out. He scanned the room, searching for Ally. Then, as everything was still, he heard a chink of a cup coming from the kitchen.

He bounced off the last step and strode across towards the kitchen to find Ally standing by the kettle which was starting to boil. She had her head resting against the wall cupboard, her eyes closed and mouth wide open as a yawn spread from corner to corner of her mouth. 'Hang on, let me just get my fishing rod, I think I could catch me a fish in there!' Ben said, trying to hide the laughter that was beginning to bubble inside.

Ally's eyes shot open. She was just about to respond as she waited and waited for something to say in response but instead her mind went blank – her brain hung a closed sign. Ally poured the boiling water into her cup as it turned from clear to a golden brown of pure delight. The aroma of the tea raised up as she took in a deep breath and let it hug every cell of her body.

Ben stood shaking his head as he watched Ally become absorbed in her cup of tea of delight. Ally lifted out the tea bag. 'I'm just going to go and do the final check' Ben said as he walked over to the fridge, got out the milk and handed it to her. Ally poured in the milk and watched it swirl. She lifted the cup and took a sip as Ben kissed her on her cheek. 'Mmm' Ally responded. 'I like to think that was for me, but I have a feeling that was aimed at your other lover' he said, pointing to the cup of tea.

Ally smiled, 'Oh no, that was definitely for you' she said sarcastically. 'Ha! I know where I am in the pecking order. I just never thought I would be second to Mr Yorkshire Tea' Ben said in jest. He slipped on his boots by the front door, opened it and disappeared into the darkness. 'I can't help it that he just hasn't perfected the art of hugs in a mug' Ally thought to herself.

She slipped the milk back into the fridge and closed the door. She picked up her cup and began to make her way across the living room towards the staircase, taking a sip of tea as she made her way. She felt the tiredness seep around her body as she took hold of the carved wooden banister and slid her hand up it as she made her way upstairs. When she reached the top she paused for a second to hear Hugh's snoring in the background. She continued on towards the bedroom.

Ally pushed open the door and ran her hand along the wall as she felt her way through the darkness. 'I must be close' she whispered to herself. 'Oh you bugger!' she yelled, followed by a slosh of tea splashing on the floor. Her toe had found the bedside table first as she reached and turned on the bedside light, quickly placing the cup on the table and flopping on the bed to nurse her toe. She rolled around grunting and groaning as her toe throbbed screaming 'Man down! Man down!'.

'Note to self – turn on the big light when entering the room' Ally muttered to herself. Downstairs she heard the front door open and close, and the thump of two boots landing on the floor. Ally gingerly hopped towards the en suite and closed the door behind her as she began to get ready for bed.

Ben stood at the bottom of the stairs and then leaped up them, taking two steps at a time. 'Two, four, six, eight' he spoke, as he continued to the top. His feet came to rest on the landing and he turned around, pointing down to the stairs. 'See, I've still got it, one nil to me!' he said as he marched, pleased with himself, towards the bedroom.

As he made his way through the bedroom door he heard Ally humming in the bathroom. He looked at the closed door. 'That must be a magical door into some kind of portal, or maybe there is a magic button that transports her to some spa or coffee shop. What could take so long?' he asked himself as he listened to her moving around. Then Ally's humming stopped. Ben began to quickly get undressed. As he placed his watch on the bedside table he felt his sock quickly absorb a liquid. He lifted it up and saw a pool of tea. 'What the…!' as he heard the bathroom door click open.

He slipped off his sock as Ally stepped out. He held it up. 'Is there something you need to tell me?' Ben asked jokingly as he got into bed. Ally sheepishly walked around to the other side of the bed. 'I may have taken on the bedside table with one of my toes.' Ben raised his eyebrows. 'And who won?' Ally climbed into bed and picked up her cup of tea and continued to look straight ahead. 'The table' she said, partly muffled by the cup. 'What was that?' Ben asked teasingly. Ally turned her head in the other direction, pretending to be disgusted. Ben chuckled to himself as he reached across and turned off the lamp. The room descended into darkness with only the moonlight cascading a pool of beautiful light on the wooden floor.

Ally took another sip of tea as she became lost in her thoughts whilst looking at the moonlight. 'Oh how much has changed since the last time I sat watching the moon travel across the sky.' She thought back to the night she booked the flights to go on an adventure with Hugh.

She placed her cup on the bedside table, slid down the bed, pulled the duvet up and took hold of Ben's hand. He intertwined his fingers with hers and rolled over to face her. Looking into her eyes, he said 'The moment was filled with magic, as our hearts combined, souls intertwined, when your lips touched mine, watching my wish come true, having my first forever kiss with you.' Ally smiled then moved across and laid her head on his chest whilst looking at the pool of moonlight. Ben kissed her goodnight.

As the morning sun began to stream in through the window, Hugh bounded into Ben and Ally's bedroom. He jumped on the bed and climbed under the duvet between Ben and Ally. Ally let out a large yawn as she rolled over to be greeted by a bright eyed and very excited Hugh. Her eyes started to focus and her mind lifted the closed sign. 'What are you so excited about?' Ally groaned. 'It's today!' Hugh said, sitting bolt upright. Ally frowned. Had she forgotten something? 'What's today?' Ally said. 'No, mom, it's just today, a whole day to create, play, make a new memory, so many opportunities' Hugh said as he flopped back down with his arms above his head.

Ben propped himself up on his elbow looking across to Ally and Hugh. Ally continued to look confused and then pulled the duvet up over her head. Ben looked at Hugh. I think someone needs a cup of tea before they're ready to start the day. 'Oh mom!' Hugh groaned. 'I'm sure you are going to turn into a tea bag one day after the amount you drink' he said, peeling himself off the bed and jumping down off the bed, his feet hitting the floor with a thump.

Ben followed on behind, picking up his clothes and pulling on his jeans and shirt. As he reached the door he looked back at the bed. 'There will be a cup of tea waiting for you at the kitchen table' he said. Ally threw back the duvet and bolted out the room, nearly knocking Ben over. She whirled down the stairs, across the living room into the kitchen and plonked herself down on the kitchen chair.

She watched Hugh place a bowl on the kitchen table, grab the cereal box and milk, and settle down to join her. Ben made his way down the stairs and into the kitchen and put the kettle on. 'Before you both disappear to go on one of your adventures…' Ally began. Hugh looked up at Ben and smiled with delight. Ally watched them both. 'Like I was saying... I have something I need to talk to you about.' 'Is it about Molly, mom?' Hugh said with a mouthful of cereal. 'What was that in English?' Ally said with a disapproving look. 'Do you need to talk to us about Molly? It's just that I had a really weird dream last night that I saw Molly running off with a rucksack and crying.' Ally glanced at Ben; Ben shrugged his shoulders.

'Yes, it's about Molly and her parents. I got an email yesterday. Do you remember Nana O?' Ally asked looking at Hugh, still not quite sure how to interpret his dream. Hugh nodded as he shovelled another spoonful of cereal into his mouth. 'Well, she has returned back to the stars and left them with some money. They are under strict instructions from her to use it to go on an adventure.' Hugh continued to chew his cereal whilst looking at Ally. 'Molly's parents had tried to get in touch with us' Ally said, looking at Hugh. 'Your Grandma told them that we were now living here in America and they asked if we would mind them paying us a visit.' Ally looked at Ben as he placed a cup of tea in front of Ally and picked up his coffee before joining them at the table.

Hugh stopped chewing and looked directly at Ally. 'When are they coming? We are going away with Sally, John and Aden in three days' time!' Hugh said looking concerned. 'Please, mom, don't cancel the trip.' 'Don't worry, Hugh, they won't be coming over that soon' Ben said reassuringly. Ally stared into her cup of tea. Ben looked across at Ally who looked a little guilty. 'When are they coming over Ally?' Ben asked, becoming more concerned.

'Well, the thing is... they kind of want to get going on their adventure so... I might have said they could come as soon as they like. They emailed back and they are arriving tomorrow' Ally said, not taking her eyes off her tea. Ben leaned back in his chair and looped his thumb through his belt with a look of disbelief. He continued to stare at Ally. 'Well, that's fine with me, they can join us when we head up to Yellowstone' Hugh responded, as he picked up his empty bowl and made his way across to the dishwasher and placed it inside. 'That's what I thought' Ally said, still looking at Ben. Ben took in a deep breath and let out a sigh. Hugh patted Ben on the shoulder as he walked past and made his way across to the front door. He slipped on his boots, lifted his coat and hat off the peg and disappeared out into the morning sunshine.

Ally's look turned to curiosity. 'What was that about?' Ally said, wafting her finger towards his shoulder. Ben took another sip of his coffee. 'What was what about?' he said dismissively, shrugging his shoulders. 'That!' Ally said, wafting her finger more vigorously at him. 'Nothing. Stop trying to change the subject. Why didn't you talk to me about it first?' Ben said calmly, trying to hide the growing sadness inside.

'I thought it would be alright' Ally said tentatively. She hadn't seen this side to Ben before. Ben pushed his chair up, placed his cup in the sink and walked towards the front door. Ally watched him in shock. 'Why was he being so off about this?' she thought to herself. Ben pulled on his boots, grabbed his hat and made his way out of the front door without saying another word.

Ally stood up and watched him shaking his head as he walked across to the barn. 'What was that all about?' Ally said aloud to herself, becoming more annoyed. She took the first step towards following him but stopped. 'Give him space' she said to herself. 'He'll tell you later. He just needs time to himself' Ally said, comforting herself.

Ally picked up her cup of tea and began to make her way back upstairs to get dressed. As she walked across the living room her thoughts whirled around like a tornado, growing as she moved through sadness, fear and anger. As she reached the stairs she turned round and sat down on the bottom step, cupping her tea in her hands. 'He's hiding something' she said to the empty room.

As she looked out of the large living room windows at the mountain on the horizon and the rolling lush green hills, she felt a warmth of love rise from deep inside. She began to feel lighter as the tornado of thoughts dissolved away. 'Don't think the worst, Ally. Good things happen every day. Maybe what he is hiding is going to be today's gift' she said to herself as she stared at the mountain.

Ally started to drift off into her own world as she thought about the first day she and Hugh came to Ben's house. She thought of how the scenery took her breath away and how she had walked down to the stream at the bottom of the garden. Whilst she had sat by the stream she recalled something she had written: 'Life is magical with its twists and turns, sometimes not knowing that happiness is awaiting us just around the next corner. If only we had the courage to seek and keep moving forward, as we watch the love that fills our life transform around us as we go' Ally whispered.

Ally sprang to her feet. 'It's all alright!' Ally said as she leaped up the stairs two by two, pacing towards her room. She placed the cup down on the bedside table, this time avoiding reaching it with her toes first. She started to get dressed. As she was pulling on her jumper Ally looked out of the bedroom window and saw that Tom had arrived. Ally made her way over to the window. She looked to see Ben and Tom looking very serious in a deep conversation as they sat on the tailgate of Tom's truck.

Ally continued to watch, intrigued. She gently opened the window so she was able to hear what they were talking about. Maybe she could figure out what had upset Ben. As the window opened she began to lean out slightly, to see Ben lift his hat off and ruffle his hair before placing his hat back on as he shook his head again.

'Mom, it's rude to listen in to other people's conversations' Hugh said, standing in the middle of the bedroom. Ally spun round in shock and glared at Hugh. 'When?... how long?...' Ally stuttered. 'I thought you were in the barn!' Ally burst out and then quickly closed the window. She stormed out of the room and Hugh followed in hot pursuit.

'Mom, why were you listening in?' Hugh persisted. Ally rapidly made her way down the stairs. 'I wasn't' she paused. 'Alright, I was, but it was just to find out why Ben's upset' Ally said, still hurrying to the kitchen to shake off her interrogator. 'Why don't you just ask him?' Hugh asked innocently. 'It's not that simple' Ally said, turning round to face Hugh. 'Yes it is, mom. Jeez, why do adults make things so complicated?' Just then, Ben and Tom walked through the front door. 'Morning Miss Ally' Tom said cheerily. 'Hi Tom, coffee?' Ally said. She glanced at Hugh, giving him a stern look meaning that he was not to say a word.

'Yes, that would be great' Tom said, pulling out a

chair and sitting down at the kitchen table. Ben made his way over to the fridge whilst Ally made a fresh pot of coffee. The stiffness of the silence seemed to fill the room. Tom looked at Hugh, motioning with his eyes between Ben and Ally with a confused look. Hugh raised up his arms to the sky 'God only knows!' he proclaimed, shaking his head.

Ben turned round looking confused and Hugh took his chance. 'Mom was eavesdropping in on your conversation' Hugh said and very quickly moved behind a kitchen chair for protection. There was a thud as they all turned to see Ally bang her head against the kitchen wall cupboard.

Ally regained her composure and put the fresh pot of coffee on the table. 'I'm going to go into town to get some more food and things for when Molly and Co arrive' she said, avoiding looking at Ben. Tom tried to stop himself bursting out into a laugh by pretended to cough. He cleared his throat as one or two chuckles escaped. 'See you in a couple of days before you head up to Yellowstone' Tom managed to say before looking down at the table. He could no longer stop himself smirking.

'People don't tell me anything' Ally said in frustration, not wanting to be the punchline to the joke anymore. She grabbed her handbag and stomped a foot into each shoe before waltzing out of the front door. She made sure she slammed it closed to emphasise her disgust. As she walked across to the truck she heard laughter begin to float through the air. This fuelled the anger inside her even more.

She got into the truck and, as she closed the door, tears of frustration rolled down her cheeks. She leaned her head against the steering wheel. As each tear escaped from inside she felt a relief as all she could hear was her breath going in and out like a rocking chair on a summer's evening. Ally looked up and wiped away the last of the tears before noticing Ben watching her through the kitchen window. Ally started the truck and pushed down hard on the accelerator. This caused the truck to roar as she stared sternly back at Ben before reversing and driving off.

Ben turned back to Tom who had finally been able to stop laughing. Tom looked up at Ben with a big grin. 'She really doesn't know does she?' he said in disbelief. Ben just shook his head. 'It will be a miracle if I am able to survive the next few days. At least there will be something to distract her and take me out of the firing line' Ben said, partly joking. Deep inside he was a little afraid as he remembered how feisty and fiery Ally was the first night they had met in the bar.

Hugh watched Ben as he smiled to himself. 'What were you thinking about just then?' Hugh asked inquisitively. Ben looked down at his boots and pretended to kick some dirt as he smiled. 'The night I met your mom. That was one of the best days I have lived so far' he said, looking at Hugh. 'Obviously what you mean to say is that it was second to the moment you met me?' Hugh said, placing his hands on his hips. 'Obviously' Ben laughed.

'So, do you think you've got everything you need to run this place whilst we're in Yellowstone?' Ben said, getting down to business. Tom swilled down the last of his coffee. 'Yes, nothing to it' he said, standing up and pushing his chair under the table. Ben walked across and held out his hand. Tom met it with his and they shook hands. Ben placed his other hand on Tom's shoulder. 'Thanks for this' he said gratefully, 'I've always got your back, always have, always will, you know that right?' Ben smiled, nodding his head.

'Maybe it's worth you getting some protective gear for when Ally comes back, just to be on the safe side' Tom said sarcastically, before he headed out the front door. Ben watched him get in his truck and drive off up the dirt road. Hugh sat patiently looking at Ben. 'So...' Hugh said slowly. 'Well, with mom out, umm, I guess, maybe, if you like' Hugh said, casually trying to hide the volcano of excitement about to burst out of him.

'Well, there is only one thing for it' Ben said 'Mucking out stalls.' Hugh put his head on the table in disgust and let out a groan. 'Or we could take a ride out to the beach if you want something a little different' Ben said, trying to keep a straight face. Hugh's head shot up 'Seriously?' he exclaimed. 'Sure' Ben said, heading over the room to put his baseball cap on.

Hugh jumped off the chair and started to dance around the kitchen. 'Oh yeah! Oh yeah!' he cheered, and dashed out the kitchen up into his bedroom to put on his swimming shorts. Ben headed into his office and picked up a rucksack. He then went back into the kitchen to fill it with snacks, drinks and towels. He then headed upstairs to put on his swimming shorts too.

As he was about to start to make his way up the stairs, Hugh came whooshing down the banister. Ben caught him at the bottom. 'Thanks!' he said, leaping out of Ben's arms and heading into the kitchen. Ben was just about to say something but Hugh was already gone.

Hugh picked up his rucksack and Ben's rucksack and proceeded to skip out of the front door into the sun. He climbed into Ben's truck, placed the rucksacks on the back seat and rested his feet on the dashboard. Ben appeared by the front door and began to make his way across to the truck. Hugh tilted his head and screwed up his eyebrows. 'Ben looks weird without his jeans and boots on' Hugh thought.

Ben opened the truck door and climbed in. He placed the key in the ignition and the truck came to life.

Hugh quickly pressed the play button on the car stereo as the speakers began to blare out 'Life is a highway, I wanna ride it all night long!' Ben burst into laughter as he started to drive up the dirt road. Hugh wiggled and bopped to the song in the seat next to him.

The car cruised down the highway towards the ocean. Ben tapped his fingers on the steering wheel to the music. Hugh was captivated by the scenery whirring by. 'I see it, I see it!' Hugh shouted as he pointed out ahead of them. There on the horizon was a sliver of ocean, growing closer by the minute. 'I do too' Ben said, humbly lost in his thoughts. Hugh looked across at him 'Why is mom so angry with you?' he asked.

Ben glanced across and gave a weak smile. 'When you find something you love most, people then spend the rest of their lives worrying about losing it and never figure out that unless they lose or change that part of themselves it will never go, that's for the good and the bad' he said.

Hugh continued to watch the ocean draw ever closer. 'So she thinks she is going to lose you? But that doesn't make any sense. You haven't said or done anything that would suggest that' Hugh said, looking puzzled. Ben nodded. 'I know that, you know that, but here's where it gets all muddled up in people's minds. Whether it's true or not, our imaginations will always win over logic, especially if the stories in our imaginations are fuelled by strong emotions. Even when they know they are being irrational they still can't stop the momentum building of all the "what ifs", fear and anger occurring in their minds' Ben said as he chewed his thumb nail.

Hugh stayed quiet as he digested what Ben was saying. 'Here's another way of looking at it: your thoughts are like waves of the ocean, they are always going to keep coming and going – that's guaranteed. But sometimes the waves will be part of a raging storm, with giant waves crashing against the shore and causing destruction. Or the waves can be big but are fun where you may go surfing, or they could be small and gentle and part of a beautiful sunset. It's the same waves coming and going but three totally different ways to experience them, the first causing fear and panic, the second fun and laughter, and maybe some lessons too, and the third bringing peace and harmony.'

Ben turned the truck down a small road where the land started to change into golden sand, as he watched Hugh thinking intently about what he had just heard. 'But...' Hugh began, as Ben pulled into the beach car park, slipped into a space and turned off the ignition. 'We don't have control of the ocean. It's huge – more than huge – gigantic! So we can't control which waves we get' Ben said, leaning on the steering wheel and looking out towards the ocean.

'That's what most people see, this uncontrollable force controlling them. However, that's not the full story. It's how you see yourself and the waves. Are you a master of the ocean or a victim? There are great sailors who have navigated the toughest of waves and storms because they saw themselves as a person who could. There are people who have had the best times of their life surfing out in the ocean because they saw themselves dancing with the waves. There are many who have walked along the water's edge with the waves lapping their toes feeling peaceful and harmonious with all parts of life' Ben continued.

'Yet there are others who have got themselves into a lot of trouble with the ocean and their imaginations because they let it be driven by their fears and, worst, "what ifs". They never take the time to change the image of what the water is reflecting back to them' Ben concluded. 'Mom has created a storm in her head from her worst fears hasn't she? Her imagination is controlling her with her fears' Hugh sighed. 'I'm afraid so' Ben smiled wearily.

Ben and Hugh stepped out of the truck and onto the golden sand which was warm from the morning's sun. As they took off their t-shirts and closed the truck doors, Hugh screamed 'Last one to the sea is rotten poo!' as he ran as fast as he could down to the water with Ben in hot pursuit.

2 THE MAN OF THE MOUNTAIN

As the truck pulled in front of the house, the headlights beamed into the kitchen window and illuminated Ally who was whirling around with plates in her hands. Ben turned off the ignition and the darkness of nightfall engulfed them, with only the porch light illuminating the path to the front door.

Ben and Hugh stepped out of the truck and grabbed the rucksacks. Hugh quickly closed his door and skipped to the front door with Ben following on behind. As they made their way in through the front door, Hugh rushed towards the kitchen. 'Mom, mom, you'll never guess where we have been!' Hugh exclaimed. Ally stopped laying the table and looked across at both of them with a look that was ice cold. Hugh ground to a halt and paused as Ben came up alongside him. Hugh saw his opportunity. 'Erm, I'm just going to have a shower before dinner' he said quickly before dashing upstairs out of the firing line.

Ben watched Ally's gaze go up and down him as he stood in his shorts and t-shirt, not saying a word but only raising one of her eyebrows in conclusion at what she saw. She then returned to laying the table. Ben turned around and headed into his office, placing his rucksack next to his desk. He plonked himself in his chair and stared at the picture of him and Ally dancing, taken from the night they first met in the bar. He began to swivel around on his office chair and tap his fingers on the chair arm, as his thoughts began to formulate a plan.

He brought the chair to a sudden stop. 'That's it!' he said, pleased with himself. He opened the top drawer of his desk, took out a notepad and ripped off three sheets of paper. He then grabbed two pens and swivelled his chair round to face the office door. 'Ally, can you come here please?' he called. Ally looked up and then continued to place the pie in the oven.

Ben remained motionless and listened to Ally intently. 'I'm busy!' Ally shouted back as she threw the oven gloves on the worktop. 'Ally!' Ben said, more sternly. Ally stormed across towards the office and was just about to vent her thoughts when Ben placed his finger on his lips, motioning for her to stay quiet. He pointed to the other chair in the office.

Ally's face turned to thunder as she stomped across

and sat down in the chair with a huff. Ben reached across with his foot and tapped the office door shut before turning his chair back to face Ally. Ally sat with her arms and legs crossed, and eyes narrowed ready for a fight. Ben picked up the piece of paper and pen and handed them to Ally. 'Ben, I don't have time for this, I have dinner to cook, the house to clean, the spare bedrooms to get ready' Ally continued, reeling off the ever growing to do list that was building in her mind. 'I know and I will help, but I think you do have time to create our future' Ben said affectionately. Ally paused and then looked away, as tears began to build.

Ben placed the pen and paper on her lap and took her hands in his. 'Just ten minutes is all I ask' he said, looking deeply into Ally's eyes. She turned and saw that same sparkle in his eyes that she had seen the night before. 'I know you are up to something. Why won't you tell me?' Ally asked with concern. 'I will when the time is right, I just need you to trust me. I'm not going anywhere, you are not going to lose me' Ben said as he tucked some of her hair behind her ear.

Ally couldn't hold the tears back anymore as, drop by drop, they landed on the piece of paper on her lap. Ben turned back to his desk and ripped off a fresh sheet of paper. He took a pack of tissues from his rucksack and handed them to Ally. Ally smiled meekly. 'Quit being so nice, I'm trying to be angry with you' she snuffled.

Ben smiled. 'I'm sure there will be many opportunities for you to practise that' he said, before spinning around and taking his piece of paper and pen. Without looking at Ally he said 'I want you to write down what your dreams are, Ally. Be honest, no matter how big they are.' Ben looked down at the blank sheet of paper before him and took a deep breath. 'It's been a long while since I've last done this' he thought as he began to write.

Ally watched Ben's pen whizz across the page as each line filled up with words. She looked down at the blank page and picked up her pen as her hand began to shake. 'I can't' Ally muttered. Ben looked up 'Say again?' Ally placed the pen back down and looked at Ben. 'I can't do this. If I don't dream then I have nothing to lose. If I have nothing to lose then I don't have to ever go through the pain and heartache of something being taken away from me again.' Ally pulled another tissue out to wipe away more tears.

Ben sat motionless, not saying a word. He looked down at his paper at all the words containing his dreams that filled the page, and the hope that filled the space in between each word. 'There's a man who lives at the bottom of the mountain. He spoke very little but took me to a mirror that hung in his house. He asked: "Who is the man on the other side of that mirror?" For the first time I truly looked at the reflection and shook my head "I don't know". The man pointed to my heart and said "Well, he's not who your mother says you are or your father, teacher, preacher or anyone else who has an opinion. He is who you say he is, what's in your heart'" Ben said.

Ben looked at Ally and said 'Are you telling me that there is no person looking back at you in the mirror? Because if that's the case then maybe you died along with Hugh's dad. But when I look at you I see a spark in your heart that wants to shine, shining bright and bringing so much love to this life.' Ally took in a deep breath. 'Just making it through the day is enough for me' Ally said softly. 'Well, I'm asking you to start creating each day instead' Ben said sympathetically.

Ally sat for a moment. In her heart she knew she couldn't keep playing the role of the walking dead, not with Ben and Hugh in her life. She picked up her pen and began to write. With each line that filled with her dreams she felt her heart lighten, the weight of her shoulders lift and a sense of joy flow around her veins.

Ben turned back to his piece of paper and, without saying another word, continued to write. The room was silent except for the faint noise of the pens flowing across the pages. As Ben reached the bottom of his page, he glanced at his list. It contained dreams he hadn't dared to dream before. He smiled to himself and turned to Ally. She sat glowing with delight as she flipped the page over and continued to write.

Ben watched and rested his head on the back of the chair, gently swivelling it from side to side with gladness. Ally's writing began to slow down as she re-read the last sentence, placed her pen down on Ben's desk and handed him the piece of paper. Ben shook his head and tapped his hand on his lap, motioning for her to come and join him. As Ally got up and sat down on Ben's lap, he pulled the third blank piece of paper towards him and wrote at the top of the page: "Our Dreams".

Ally smiled as she kissed his cheek. 'You know sometimes you are just amazing.' Ben blushed in response. Ally placed her piece of paper of dreams on the left and Ben slid his piece of paper of dreams on the right. Ally read out the first of her dreams followed by Ben reading out the first of his, and then together they wrote down their combined dreams. They continued to sit in the serenity of the evening as they wrote down their dreams line by line, combining each of their dreams and creating their life.

Ben lifted the final piece of paper up and looked into Ally's eyes. No words were spoken but everything was said. All of a sudden Ally was brought back to reality. 'The pie!' she screamed as she jumped up, opened the office door and then fell over Hugh who had been secretly listening on the other side of the door. They both lay on the floor in fits of laughter. Ben walked over and lifted them both back to their feet. Ally continued on her way, staggering with laughter as she grabbed the oven gloves, opened the oven and took out the pie. By this time it was beginning to turn black.

She placed it on the side and crouched back down as she couldn't stop herself from laughing. This new sense of freedom she felt was electrifying. Hugh dusted himself off, turned to Ben and hugged him. 'Thank you' he whispered. Ben leaned over and kissed Hugh on the top of his head. 'I think everything is going to be ok' he said as they walked across to sit down at the kitchen table.

Ally stood back up, wiped away the tears of joy and began to dish up the dinner. Hugh looked at Ally. 'Thanks, mom' as Ally placed some pie on his plate. 'Do I get to know what you two were doing in the office?' Hugh asked before putting a large piece of pie into his mouth. Ally sat down and joined them at the table. 'We were making our own vision wall of a sort' Ally said, smiling across to Ben. Ben was caught navigating putting a very large piece of pie in his mouth.

'Do you think we could make a family vision wall?' Hugh asked, looking at Ben and then across to Ally. 'Do you know what, Hugh? That's a great idea!' Ben said with enthusiasm. The atmosphere suddenly began to feel heavy. 'Not tonight though, I have got enough to do' Ally said as she started to remember her job list. 'How can we help?' Ben asked, glancing across to Ally. 'Well, for starters, you two can stop trying to have a contest of who can fit the biggest piece of pie in your mouth' Ally said, disapprovingly.

Hugh smirked. 'I just need to dust and hoover and put out some fresh towels. If you wouldn't mind washing up the dinner pots.' Ally felt the weight of life begin to creep back in. 'And Hugh you're to get an early night. We have a busy few days ahead of us and the last thing I need is for you to be grumpy because you're tired.' Hugh was just about to dispute the last part but felt a nudge from Ben under the table. He looked across and Ben winked with acknowledgement. 'No problem, mom' Hugh begrudgingly agreed.

Ally got back up from the table. 'Don't you want your dinner?' Ben asked, concerned. 'I'm not hungry. I'm just going to get on and get an early night too, I think...' Ally stopped herself 'Nevermind' as she placed her plate next to the sink before disappearing upstairs into the spare bedroom.

'Why do I get the feeling that there is a bit more to the story about why Molly is coming over?' Hugh said as he filled his plate with a second helping of pie. 'You and me both' Ben agreed, staring blankly in the direction Ally had just gone. 'Will it spoil your surprise?' Hugh asked. Ben shook his head, 'It will happen at the right time in the right place.'

Ben got up from the table and started to fill the sink with water. As the sound of the water echoed around the room he got a feeling inside that change was on the way. He felt that a storm was brewing and it was heading straight for them. 'Hugh, can you make a start on the pots whilst I just go and do the final check?' Hugh guzzled the last of the pie that was on his plate and joined Ben at the sink. 'Sure thing' said Hugh. Ben ruffled his hair and walked across to the front door where he slid on his boots and headed outside.

Hugh stood motionless at the sink as a shiver went down his spine. 'That's odd' he said to himself as the room began to feel cold. Hugh shook his body to dislodge the feeling and started to wash the pots one by one. As the bubbles and water splashed, Hugh mused 'I wonder if it's going to be weird with Molly being here? What if she doesn't like adventures. Oh no! What if she just wants to sit and watch TV?' Hugh's expression began to change as, for the first time, he became worried. 'Just stop' he said loudly to himself. Then he remembered what Ben had said earlier about the ocean.

'I choose to have fun' Hugh said, breathing a sigh of relief. Just then he heard the front door open as Ben returned, took off his boots and joined Hugh in the kitchen. Hugh placed the last plate on the draining board and turned to face Ben who was already wiping down the table. 'Who's the man at the bottom of the mountain?' he blurted out.

Ben paused as he thought what to say before continuing to wipe. 'He is just someone who was part of my life. We'll leave it at that' he said as he placed the dish cloth back by the sink and silently headed into his office.

Hugh stood startled. Ben had never not told him something or kept a secret. Hugh trudged his way across the living room and slowly climbed the stairs step by step, pulling himself up by the banister. As he went he felt all his dreams start to be undone, stitch by stitch. As he reached the top he was greeted by Ally buzzing round the spare room.

'Hugh, could you tidy your room before you get ready for bed?' Ally called from inside the room. Hugh continued to look at the wooden floor as he slowly made his way into his room and closed the door behind him. 'What was happening? Why did everything feel out of sync?' Hugh mused. He really wanted to ask Ben more about the man at the bottom of the mountain, but for the first time ever he didn't feel he could talk to him.

Hugh started to pick his clothes up off the floor and

put them in the wash basket. He then stacked his magazines at the bottom of his wardrobe. He turned on his bedside lamp and changed into his pj's, climbed under his duvet and lay on his side looking up at his vision wall. He looked up at the different pictures and felt for the first time that he didn't believe.

There was a gentle tap on his door. Hugh stayed silent as he heard it begin to creek open. Hugh continued to look up at the wall as Ben's head appeared in the gap. 'Can I come in?' he whispered. 'If you want to' Hugh said numbly. Ben walked in and closed the door behind him. 'Scoot up' Ben said as he laid down next to Hugh.

'Sorry about that earlier, son, it's just not a story I'm ready to tell' said Ben. Hugh turned over and faced Ben, looking at him intensely. Hugh's expression began to soften as he knew Ben wouldn't usually keep something from him. 'That's ok, I understand' Hugh said lovingly as he hugged Ben. 'You are a miracle, you know that right?' Ben said, wrapping his arms around Hugh. 'Everything feels out of alignment. The last time it felt like this was when dad had died' Hugh said nervously. Ben pulled him in closer towards his chest, 'Did you hear me talking to your mom about the mirror?' Ben asked. 'No, of course not, I wasn't listening in' Hugh said sheepishly. Ben gave him a sideways glance. 'Well maybe a little bit' Hugh confessed. 'That sounds more like the truth' Ben said, chuckling. 'Sometimes those two people in the mirror disagree. One may see greatness whilst the other is blinded by fear. Part of us is asking us to believe in something that no one else can see yet and you may begin to doubt if you can be that person. That's when you become uncomfortable as the conflict grows before you take a leap of faith and take the action needed to move from one form to the next. Maybe you have changed your question and you're seeking something else to learn about life? So life is saying that you need to start to move your feet, explore and find the truth. Just like you did with the vision wall. It doesn't mean you have taken a step back. If you look at a circle from above it just looks like you are going round and round in circles. However, if you look at it from a different perspective – from the side – you see that each time you have come full circle you have actually spiralled up a level' Ben finished.

Hugh pondered the thought. 'I think you're right. I want to understand more and I think it starts with the man at the bottom of the mountain.' His body began to tingle as soon as he said it aloud. Ben shuffled uncomfortably 'I know. It's just hard for me to accept that right now, but I won't stand in your way'. Ben kissed Hugh goodnight and sat up on the bed looking out into the room. 'Many nights I sat in this room dreaming that it would be filled with life and love, with a person curious and courageous, and here you are' Ben said as he turned and looked at Hugh.

Ben stood up and made his way to the door, opened it and stepped out onto the landing. 'Night night, Ben' Hugh said as he snuggled under his duvet. 'Night night, Champion' Ben said warmly as he closed the door and walked towards the bedroom.

Ben turned on the bedside lamp, undressed and climbed into bed. He listened as he heard Ally's footsteps coming up the stairs. Ben lay in bed with his arms folded above his head, lost in thought, as he stared out of the window at the moon thinking about Hugh and where he was going to go next. Ally walked around to the other side of the bed and placed her cup of tea on the bedside table. She quickly changed into her pj's and joined Ben. She stared as she watched a sombre expression creep over his face.

'Is everything ok?' Ally asked. Ben snapped out of his dream, coughing to clear his throat. 'Yes' he replied dismissively as he reached and switched off the bedside lamp. Ally reached for her tea and as she slowly took a sip she looked out of the window at the stars. She glanced across as she heard Ben begin to breathe deeply as he had already fallen asleep. Ally climbed back out of bed taking her tea and walked around the bed and across the landing on her tip toes, trying not to wake everyone.

As she reached the stairs she took each step slowly, lowering herself as she made her way downstairs, pausing each time the wood under her feet creaked. Ally walked across to the couch, lifted the blanket that was lying on the back of it and made her way across to the door. She opened it and walked out onto the back porch. As she stepped outside she shivered with the cool night air. She quickly walked across to the bench that looked out onto the mountain and the stunning landscape.

She could hear the horses moving around in the field and a coyote howl in the distance. Ally sat down on the bench and wrapped the blanket tightly around her, taking another sip of tea, whilst staring blankly out towards the hills which were lit by the moonlight on this clear, starry night. Ally took in a deep breath. As the cool air filled her lungs she shivered and pulled the blanket around tighter.

As Ally sat, her mind was still but her heart was full of fear. Ally lowered her cup and placed it on the ground. She brought her legs up onto the bench and laid down. She looked at the mountain. 'I don't want to be afraid and feel helpless anymore' she whispered as the tears silently rolled down her cheeks.

The silence of the evening continued to fill the air. As Ally stared at the stars, a feeling began to grow inside that somehow the stars were protecting and guiding her. Ally felt the weight of life begin to lift again, as the silence in nature began to soothe her, dissolving away her worries, lightening her heart and smothering her fear. Then the tiredness set in as Ally's eyes began to droop and started to close. Just as she was about to fall asleep she watched an owl fly by, heading towards the mountain. 'Hello Nana O' she muttered, before sleep finally took over.

As the morning sunlight rose it shined a beam of light through the window that cascaded onto Ben's face. He began to stir; as he rolled over and stretched out his arm he found an empty space. He slowly opened his eyes and glanced around the room – there was no sign of Ally. He pulled back the duvet and placed his feet on the floor. He rubbed his face with his hands as he adjusted to the morning light.

He stood up and reached for his jeans and shirt, pulled them on and shuffled down the landing with his body still heavy from its slumber. He glanced over the banister but there was still no sign of Ally. His heart began to race as he rushed down the stairs and into the kitchen. 'Ally!' he cried, as he turned and scanned the living room. He saw the patio doors slightly open and he ran across the living room, his bare feet pounding on the wooden floor as he headed out onto the back porch. As he stared out onto the land he glanced to his left and saw Ally curled up on the bench with the blanket draped over her.

He placed his hands on his head as he took in a big

breath of life and looked across towards the mountain. The fire in his heart, fuelled by the love he felt, began to settle. He walked across to the bench and lifted Ally up into his arms as he sat down on the bench next to her. Ally began to stir, let out a large yawn and rubbed her eyes. She saw the fear in Ben's eyes. She suddenly sat up. 'What's wrong?' she asked, confused. Ben cupped her head in his hands as they had a kiss of life.

'I thought you had gone' he said, looking straight into her eyes. Ally's face looked even more confused. 'No, I just needed to be close to the stars, to family' she stuttered. 'It's hard to explain' she said, shaking her head. Ben turned round and sat back against the bench as Ally moved in closer to him and rested her head on his chest. As they sat watching the sun continuing to rise, the moment filled with a sense of magic.

'We'd better get ready, you'll need to be heading to the airport soon' Ben said standing up, having savoured the moment. Ally had one last look at the countryside. 'Thank you' she whispered before standing up and following Ben inside. Ally placed the blanket on the back of the couch. 'I'm just going to have a shower and get dressed' she said, pointing to the stairs. Ben stood looking at Ally, in awe at what stood before him. 'How about pancakes this morning?' he asked, bringing himself out of a daze.

'YES, please!' Hugh shouted from the top of the stairs before bounding down them with a spring in his step.

'Morning, mom' he said as he hugged Ally. 'Morning, monkey' Ally responded. 'We're gonna have pancakes, yummy, yummy pancakes' Hugh sang as he skipped into the kitchen. Ben turned on his heels and followed Hugh as Ally made her way up the stairs. 'English or American style?' Hugh said, holding up the plain flour in one hand and pancake mixture in the other. 'Let's go English' Ben said, pointing to the plain flour. Hugh placed the packets on the worktop before his head disappeared into the cupboard as he reached and brought out a bowl.

'OK, we need a mug, eggs, milk and flour' Hugh instructed as he placed the bowl next to the flour. Ben twirled around to turn on the radio and the room filled with the sound of country music. He headed over to the fridge and returned with the eggs and milk. 'So, one cup of flour' as Hugh recalled and poured the flour into a cup, with some sprinkling on the worktop, before tipping the cup into the bowl. 'One egg' he continued, cracking it against the side of the bowl and watching it gloop into the middle of the flour. 'Finally, a cup and a half of milk' as he began to fill the cup with milk and then emptied it into the bowl. Hugh paused, scanning the kitchen. Ben walked across to the drawer, pulled out the whisk and handed it to Hugh. 'Why thank you' Hugh said in a pretend posh voice.

'You can sort out the frying pan and oil' Hugh said, wafting his hand towards Ben. Ben stomped his foot whilst making a salute sign with his hand 'Yes, sir!' he called. 'OK, next we need to take three quarters of a cupful of the mixture, pour it in there, and ta-dah!' Ben and Hugh watched as the room began to fill with the smell of pancakes.

'Something smells good' Ally said as she entered the kitchen. Ben pulled out three plates, placed them on the table and reached across for the syrup. 'First one done. Go, go, go!' Hugh screamed with excitement. Ben lifted the pan and slid the pancake onto a plate, whilst Hugh hovered with another cup of mixture. Ally took the plate, poured syrup on top of the pancake and rolled it up. She glanced at the clock on her phone, surprised at the time, and quickly got up.

'I'd better be making tracks' Ally said as she walked round the table and kissed Hugh on the top of his head. 'You haven't lost your touch, monkey' Ally remarked, waving the pancake in the air. 'See you soon' Ally said as she passed Ben. 'Love you' Ben said, giving her a kiss as she went by. Ally grabbed the car keys and headed out the front door. 'Quick, quick! Less smooching, more action!' Hugh ordered, motioning for the next pancake to be put on the plate.

'I'm on it' Ben said, springing into action as Hugh began to prepare the final pancake. Ben watched, lost in thought, as the mixture began to change colour. Hugh took the spatula as he started to slide across the kitchen, dancing and singing to the music. Ben lifted the pan and placed the pancake on the plate. 'Yahoo!' Hugh called as he leaped to his seat and pulled the plate close to him.

As Ally drove, the countryside whirled by and her thoughts began to drift back to the email she had received from Molly. There was something that wasn't being said as she recalled the last time she had seen the three of them. Ally pulled into the airport and weaved through the spaces before parking under the "Arrivals" sign. Ally sat in the car, anxiously tapping her fingers on the steering wheel. She watched the minutes slowing tick by on the car clock.

There was a gentle tap on the car window. Ally's heart skipped a beat out of fright as she looked across to see Molly's dad standing there. Ally opened the door and stepped out 'Jeez, you scared me half to death!' she said as she hugged Molly's dad. 'Well, you looked like you were on a different planet. Some things don't change' he said, standing back as Molly sprung up between them. 'Remember me?' she said excitedly. 'How could I forget?!' Ally said affectionately. 'I have one just like you back home and just as bouncy' Ally said, admiring the bright eyed girl before her.

'Hello, stranger' a voice said from behind. Ally spun round and beamed. 'Hello to you too' she said, embracing Molly's mum. 'Long time, no see. I'm still waiting on that call back you were just getting around to doing' Molly's mum said jokingly, as she squeezed Ally tighter and had a feeling of relief. Ally looked up at Molly's mum and her expression asked 'Is everything alright?' Ally asked the question with just a look. Molly's mum gave a weak smile as her eyes sparkled with a tear.

'I'll put these in the back' Molly's dad said, interrupting the moment as he pointed to the suitcases. 'Yes, that'll be great' Ally said, stepping back. 'Right you, hop in' she said, opening the door for Molly to climb into the back of the truck, followed by her mum. Ally closed the door and stepped into the driver's seat. She was greeted by Molly's dad who was already in the passenger seat.

'Right, let's head back. There is one very excited Hugh wanting to see you again, Molly' Ally said, looking at Molly in her rear view mirror. Ally turned on the ignition and quickly drove off. As the truck rolled down the highway, Molly's mum leaned forward between the two front seats. 'So, this is where you have been hiding!' she exclaimed as she watched the vast countryside pass by. Ally smiled 'Well, the adventure I went on brought with it a surprise, a good one.' 'Don't you mean a good looking one' Molly's dad said, elbowing her teasingly.

Ally began to blush 'Life's good, actually it's really good.' 'So I see' Molly's mum said, 'You're glowing' before sitting back in her seat. Ally made a right turn as they began to drive down the dirt track. 'Wow, you live in heaven' Molly said, looking out the car window, seeing the forest on one side and the open fields on the other. 'Are there horses?' Molly asked, flinging herself forward. 'Can I go riding, dad?' Molly pleaded. 'You'll have to ask Ally.' Ally quickly responded 'I think Hugh has got some things sorted for you two to do together and I think you might be one very lucky girl and get to ride his horse, Firefly' Ally said as she wound down the window to let the smell of the countryside breeze through the truck.

Ally pulled up in front of the house and parked the truck. 'Well, this is home' said Ally. Molly's mum and dad sat speechless in awe of the stunning log cabin before them. Molly unclipped her seatbelt, opened the door and ran towards the front door, which had already started to open. Hugh stepped out as Molly flung her arms around him. Hugh stumbled, hugged her back and said 'Welcome home, Molly.'

3 TWO HEARTS COMBINE AS ONE HEART DIVIDES

Ally and Molly's parents joined Hugh and Molly at the front door as Ben appeared. 'Hi, welcome' Ben said, holding out his hand and shaking Molly's dad's hand. 'It's a beautiful place you have here' Molly's dad said, admiring the stunning house before him. Ally received an approving nudge off Molly's mum as Ben stepped forward. 'Hi, nice to meet you' he said, kissing her on the cheek. 'So, you're the man who brought Ally back to life?' Molly's mum said, stepping back and looking him up and down.

Ben smiled and blushed as he turned and headed back into the house, followed quickly by Hugh and Molly. 'Come on, Molly, I'll show you where you're sleeping. You are in the room next to mine' Hugh said, tugging Molly's suitcase across the living room floor. Molly skipped behind and twirled around as she admired the living room and large patio doors framing the incredible view. Hugh pulled the suitcase up the stairs as Molly pushed from underneath as they slowly climbed.

With one final heave they lifted the suitcase onto the landing where Hugh continued to pull it into the spare room. 'This is your room, Molly' Hugh said with his arms outstretched. Molly ran and jumped on the bed, flopping down. 'It's perfect' she sang. 'Quick, follow me' Hugh said, motioning with his hands as they ran into Hugh's room next door. 'This is my room' he said, standing in the centre of the room.

Molly wandered over towards the vision wall. 'What's this?' she said, pointing to the pictures. 'Oh, this is my vision wall of the people I want to meet, the places I want to go and the dreams I want to come true. It really works too, it's the same thing I did when we came on our first trip to America' Hugh said, climbing onto his bed. Molly stepped up to join him to have a closer look at the pictures.

'That's so cool' she muttered. 'We can make one in your room if you like' Hugh said eagerly. 'OK' Molly said, bouncing off the bed onto the floor. 'But first let me show you around' Hugh said, joining her and then running out of the room. They both flew down the stairs, skidded across the living room floor and crashed into the kitchen table, where they found everyone sitting around with a fresh cup of tea.

'Mom, can we go outside so I can show Molly around the barn and meet Firefly?' Hugh asked, dancing up and down on the spot. 'Just let Molly catch her breath first, calm down a little' Ally said. Molly took a large, dramatic breath in and then let out a large sigh. 'All done' Molly said, equally as enthusiastic as Hugh. 'Go on then, let Molly borrow some of your boots and a jacket though' Ally called as Hugh and Molly darted towards the front door. 'You can have these ones' Hugh said, thrusting a pair of boots at Molly. Molly slipped on Hugh's boots and quickly followed him out of the front door.

'It's like they have never been apart' Molly's dad said, pleased. The room started to fill with an awkwardness. Ben looked at Ally uncomfortably. 'So, I thought you three could join us as we are going up to Yellowstone to visit some friends' Ally said, trying to lighten the mood. Molly's mum took a deep breath in and stared into her cup. 'We'll have to see how things go' she said as she glanced up at Molly's dad.

Ben placed his cup on the worktop, sensing more needed to be said. 'I'm just going to check Hugh isn't running circles around Molly' Ben said, making his way out of the kitchen and disappearing out of the front door. Ally watched him leave as the front door clicked closed. Ally looked back at Molly's mum. 'I'm so sorry to hear about Nana O, it must have been such a shock' Ally said sympathetically.

Molly's dad sat back in his chair and readjusted his legs under the table. 'Well, she did it in style that's for sure. When we got to her house she had already got rid of everything apart from a box of stuff for each of us and a note, which is one of the reasons we are on this trip' he continued. 'That woman knew things about life that the rest of us are still trying to figure out' Ally said. 'Hang on, what do you mean one of the reasons?' Ally asked suspiciously.

Molly's mum shuffled uncomfortably in her seat. 'There has been something on the cards and we have been trying to fix it for Molly's sake but, actually, it's just making things worse' she said. Molly's dad started to swill his tea around in his cup. Molly's mum continued. 'Molly doesn't know yet but we are' she paused 'well, we're getting a divorce.' Ally was speechless and looked at each of them in turn. 'Talk about dropping a bombshell' Ally said in disbelief. 'We wanted to come on this trip for Molly, and to honour Nana O's wish' Molly's mum said tearfully.

'Right, erm I guess, well, well to be honest I don't know what to say' Ally said shaking her head, trying to come to terms with it. 'When are you going to tell Molly?' she asked. 'After the trip, we think' Molly's mum said, looking across to Molly's dad who nodded in agreement. 'We would be thankful if you didn't say anything to her' Molly's dad joined in. 'Yes, of course, I'll keep my lips sealed' Ally said, looking out of the kitchen window watching Ben make his way back towards the front door.

Molly's mum reached over and took Ally's hand. 'We are so glad to see you happy again, Ally.' Ally smiled as she watched Ben walk through the door. 'Miracles do happen' Ally said, looking at Ben. 'And Hugh seems to be following in Nana O's footsteps' Ally said, looking back at Molly's mum and raising her eyebrows. 'Then we have double trouble because Molly's like a dog with a fresh scent after Nana O told her the story about the locket' Molly's mum smiled.

'I used to love that story' Ally said, remembering sitting by the fire. 'What story's that?' Ben asked, sitting down and joining everyone at the table. 'How did it go?' Ally said, looking up at the ceiling as she reminisced. 'Love is the answer, wishes come true, as you find the place that connects me and you' Ally recalled. Molly's mum and dad smiled with agreement. 'Huh?' Ben said, letting the words sink in.

'Is this the story about a locket someone found and those words were written on a note inside?' Ben asked inquisitively. They all looked at him in disbelief. Molly's mum was the first to break the silence. 'Yes, how do you know that?' she said, puzzled. 'My dad used to tell me a story just like that' Ben said, tapping his fingers on the table. 'What a coincidence' Molly's mum said looking from Ben to Ally and back to Ben again.

They were interrupted by a large bang as the front door flew open and a horse's head peered through it. 'Can Molly and I go for a ride?' Hugh asked, as his head appeared alongside. 'Out! No horses in the house!' Ally yelled. She watched the horse's head disappear outside which was then replaced by Molly and Hugh. Ben looked down, trying to hide his laughter.

'A quick ride down the dirt road and back. It'll be dinner time soon' Ally said grudgingly. 'Thanks, mom' Hugh replied, elated. 'Thank you, Ally' Molly said, as she pulled Hugh back outside by his shirt. Molly's dad looked across at Ally, concerned. 'Will they be safe?' he asked. Ben stood up 'Yeah, Firefly will take care of them' he smiled, still chuckling to himself.

Ally stood up. 'Let me show you where you'll be sleeping so you can get settled in' she said as she placed her cup in the sink and walked over to the suitcases that Ben had already started to pick up. Molly's mum and dad rose from the table and began to follow Ally and Ben. 'I'll light a log fire after dinner' Ben said as he made his way up the stairs. 'That'll be a good idea' Ally said. He turned to look at her as she gave him a weak smile. 'Some trip, hey?' he said, as his gut feelings were confirmed. 'Something like that' Ally responded, disheartened.

Molly's mum and dad made their way up the stairs to join Ally and Ben who were placing the suitcases in the spare room. 'We'll leave you to get settled in' Ben said, as he gentled guided Ally out of the room. 'Just don't unpack too much as we'll be heading to Yellowstone tomorrow' Ally said, leaning against the door frame with Ben standing behind her.

Molly's mum sat down on the bed as she glanced up at Molly's dad. 'To be honest, we were kind of hoping that Molly could go with you three. It'll give us chance to sort out all the paperwork and make some decisions' said Molly's mum. 'You really are being serious?' Ally said, still shocked. 'Yes' Molly's dad said, placing his hands on his hips.

'Sure, we're happy to help as much as possible' Ben said, placing his hand on Ally's shoulders. Ally took a step back and smiled at both of them, saying 'Absolutely, anything you need' as she and Ben turned around, making their way down the stairs. As they stepped off the last step, Ben took hold of Ally's hand and led her across to his office. As they walked through into the room he slowly closed the door.

Ally walked across and slowly lowered herself into his chair. 'I can't believe it. Where has this come from? What about Molly? It's going to hit her hard' Ally began rolling off the questions that were rapidly flowing around her head. Ben walked across and perched on the edge of his desk next to Ally. 'They must have their reasons and it doesn't seem like it's been a hasty decision. Molly looks like a strong girl, she'll be ok' Ben said encouragingly.

Ally swivelled her chair towards him and looked up. 'You framed them!' she said, spotting the three pieces of paper that were now hanging above his desk with the photo of them together. Ben looked around and smiled. 'Of course!' he said, pointing to the middle piece of paper entitled "Our Dreams". 'That is what I'm creating every day' he said. Ally stood up, wrapped her arms around his neck and said 'Me too.'

'I kind of feel guilty that our life together is just beginning whilst Molly's parents' is ending' Ally said, staring at the pieces of paper. 'It's not ending, Ally, it's transforming. Sometimes people have to move on to be able to move forward. You should be able to understand that.' Ally nodded in agreement. 'You're right, at least Molly has Hugh to talk to' Ally said, becoming lost in thought.

'Hmm I think we have two very adventurous kids on our hands, two seekers' Ben said humbly. Ally looked across to him 'What do you mean?' she said. 'Well, the saying "two peas in a pod" definitely applies, and those two are definitely from the same pod, and they want to find answers, the truth' Ben said keenly. 'Oh boy, I could only just about keep up with Hugh and his questions and adventures' Ally smiled, remembering when she had first brought the plane tickets.

'Well, Hugh has already started asking his next question' Ben began. 'We are going to have to make a stop off before we head up to Yellowstone. There is someone Hugh wants to meet and someone I want you to meet' Ben said, wrapping his arms around Ally's waist. Ally looked out of the office window to the mountain, standing so boldly against the countryside. 'The man at the bottom of the mountain' she whispered.

'Who is he? And how did he know the story about the locket?' Ally asked inquisitively. 'And you think Hugh asks a lot of questions!' Ben said, standing up to kiss her before exiting the office. Ally continued to look at the mountain. 'I'm guessing it has something to do with why you talk in riddles' she called back.

Ally made her way towards the kitchen as she hummed a tune, before crouching down to get out the pans to cook dinner. Ben reappeared and said 'I'll just check the kids are ok and finish up for the night' before heading out to the barn. As Ally stood back up she turned round to respond but he had already gone. Ally started to chop the vegetables and put the meat in the stew pot. 'Is there anything I can do to help?' Ally looked up to see Molly's mum standing next to the table. 'He's just taking a nap' Molly's mum pointed upstairs, in the direction of where Molly's dad was.

'Keeping me company would be a great help' Ally

smiled. Molly's mum watched as Molly and Hugh rode past the kitchen window on Firefly with Ben walking alongside carrying a sack of feed. 'Ally, life sure has turned around for you' Molly's mum said, sitting down at the table. Ally glanced out the window at Hugh and Molly laughing. 'It hasn't been easy, that's for sure' Ally replied. 'Healing never is, it's something that most of us aren't brave enough to even attempt. You are a true inspiration, Ally' Molly's mum said proudly.

Ally walked across to the cooker and placed the stew in the oven. 'To be honest, if it wasn't for Hugh I don't know if I could have done it. If he hadn't followed his intuition we wouldn't be here now. I don't know where he gets his fearlessness from' Ally said proudly.

'But like Ben said, I can now create each day and not just survive it. It's not like the journey got easier but the faith in the footsteps I take forward gets stronger which pulls me through the stormy days' Ally said, as she joined Molly's mum at the table. 'How about you, how are you doing?' Ally asked softly.

Molly's mum ran her fingers through her hair. 'Honestly, I don't know at the moment. When I'm not feeling numb I'm terrified and when I'm not terrified I feel like my heart has been frozen and then smashed with a sledge hammer into a thousand pieces, and when I'm not feeling that, the pain is so intense' Molly's mum said as tears began to well up.

Ally reached over and hugged her. 'All I know is that something deep inside me says it's the right choice. I have no clue of what is going to happen next, I just know that staying there isn't what I should do' Molly's mum said through the tears. 'Sometimes the right thing to do isn't the easiest. It's usually the hardest. No matter what happens, I'm here for you and I believe in you and you're the brave one for following that voice in your heart. I wouldn't worry about Molly. There is no better lesson than to show her it's OK to take your own path and do what's best for you' Ally replied, squeezing Molly's mum tighter.

Molly's mum sat back up and wiped away the tears. 'These aren't quite the circumstances in which I wanted us to meet back up' she smiled. 'Heck, if Nana O was here she'd have a fresh pot brewing, the biscuits out, telling us a story where miracles happens every day' Ally said joyously, wiping away one of Molly's mum's tears.

Ally got up from the table and headed over to the cupboard. She stood on her tiptoes and tried to grab something from the top shelf. 'Nearly there, come a little bit closer' she muttered. 'Ah, got it!' Ally exclaimed. As she lifted down a teapot and placed it on the table. 'Let's do this Nana O style' Ally said, as she strutted over to get two cups and put the kettle on.

Molly's mum watched Ally as she made the tea, put some biscuits on a plate and brought them over to the table. 'Who is this new Ally?' she chuckled. 'I hate to admit it but Nana O was right – love is the answer, wishes do come true. The moment I met Ben, and after a few wobbles, life transformed beyond recognition because I allowed love back into my life, but not only that, I let it fill every inch of my life. When I look in the mirror I see someone I only dreamed of becoming, but now when I look I realise I am her.' Ally said humbly whilst she poured the tea.

Molly's mum picked up the cup. 'I hope I have the same luck on the next part of my journey' she said. 'I have a feeling we are being helped and guided in ways we don't quite understand' Ally said, shaking her head in disbelief. 'Cheers to Nana O and how wonderful she was, even though her ways were sometimes a little weird' Ally said, raising her cup of tea. The two cups clinked. 'Cheers!' Molly's mum said with hope.

'I don't suppose there is another one going for me?' a voice said behind them. Ally and Molly's mum looked up to see Molly's dad standing there. 'Sure, take a seat' Ally said, as she fetched another cup. Molly's dad sat down at the table. 'I think we should tell Molly this evening and then at least she has chance to ask us thousands of questions' Molly's dad suggested. Molly's mum let out a sigh 'I guess you're right.' Ally poured a cup of tea and passed it to Molly's dad.

'She'll be alright after she gets over the shock of it. She looks like she has the courage of a hero' Ally said encouragingly. 'Miss Independent more like' Molly's dad smiled, as he took a sip of tea.

They listened and heard Molly and Hugh talking as they made their way across from the barn to the house. 'But how can that be? And why three times?' Molly asked Hugh enthusiastically. 'I don't know, it just always seems to work' Hugh said, shrugging his shoulders. They walked through the front door, kicked off their boots and headed over to the sink to wash their hands.

'How long until dinner, mom?' Hugh asked, whilst splashing Molly with water. 'Hey!' Molly screamed in disgust. 'As soon as I lay the table' Ally said, getting up and moving the teapot and plate of biscuits to the worktop. Ben stepped through the front door and headed straight to the cupboard. He brought the plates across and began setting the table as Ally lifted the stew out of the oven and placed it in the centre of the table.

'I'm so hungry' Molly said, sitting down and starting to put the stew on her plate. 'Hey, leave some for us!' Hugh said with fear as he watched Molly continue to place spoonful after spoonful of stew onto her plate. 'I'm a growing girl!' Molly said jokingly.

As they all sat around the table, Molly's dad looked

across at Molly's mum with a suggestive look. Molly's mum quickly shook her head. 'So how was Firefly, Molly?' she asked. 'Oh my goodness, mum, she is amazing. I'm going to get a horse when I get back.' 'Now hold on a minute! Where are you going to keep it?' Molly's dad asked, worried. 'In the garden' Molly said casually.

'Molly, horses need a place they can walk around and plenty of grass' Ben said, trying to ease the situation. 'Fine, I'll ask a farmer to use his field' Molly said firmly. Ben looked up from his dinner at Molly. He couldn't disagree with that idea he thought as he took another mouthful of stew. As Ben continued to stare at Molly, there was something he recognised about her. Her fieriness seemed familiar. 'She reminds me of someone but I just can't put my finger on it' Ben thought to himself.

'What time are we heading off to Yellowstone tomorrow, mom?' Hugh asked, as he sorted out the carrots from the stew and moved them to the edge of his plate. 'After you have eaten your carrots' Ally said, watching him. 'Oh, mom, that's not fair!' Hugh pleaded. 'Well, I think Firefly would be very jealous of you right now getting all those carrots' Ben stepped in. Hugh looked up at him astonished and then started to chew on a carrot whilst pulling a face of disgust.

'We'll set off tomorrow morning. There is somewhere

we need to stop on our way' Ben said, trying to hide his smile. Hugh shot a look across to him but remained motionless. 'Your mom's right though, we can't go unless your dinner is all eaten up' Ben continued. Hugh began to frantically shovel the remaining pieces of food into his mouth, including the carrots. With his mouth overflowing, 'Finished!' he spluttered.

Ben looked across to Ally, shrugging his shoulders. 'I tried' he said, placing his fork down on his empty plate. Ally got up and collected everyone's plates, placing them by the side of the sink. 'We all have' she said mockingly, ruffling Hugh's hair as she walked past. 'Right, Hugh and Ben, you're both with me. We've got the final check to do' Ally said, pulling on her boots. 'But, mom, what about…' Hugh asked. But before he could finish, Ally looked at him sternly which was her way of saying that he shouldn't say the last word. 'OK' he said, hanging his head as he got off his chair and shuffled across to where Ally was waiting.

Ben got up and joined them as Molly's mum watched the three of them step outside into the darkness. 'Mum, why couldn't I go with them?' Molly asked as she watched them through the kitchen window. Molly's dad reached across and took Molly's hand. 'Your mum and I need to speak to you about something.' Molly turned and looked at them. 'What?

About you two splitting up?' Molly said, resting her head on the back of the chair and continuing to stare out of the window.

Molly's mum and dad stared at each other in disbelief. 'You two have been acting weird for months and, mum, you are so angry all the time. When I was last with Nana O it was like she knew something was wrong and that's when she explained it all to me' Molly said, turning round and facing her parents. 'Oh, of course she did' Molly's mum said, rubbing her forehead in relief.

'What did she say?' Molly's dad asked, curious to know. Molly looked down at the table. 'That sometimes in life paths cross and combine and, just like a railway track, two paths travel side by side and make a whole one. But sometimes the railway splits up and one set of tracks goes one way and the other set of tracks goes the other way. It's not my fault that they have gone in different directions' Molly said, looking at both of her parents. 'She also said that it is better to have two happy parents that are living their own lives with me being part of both of them than one unhappy family' Molly finished.

'We still love you. This is between me and your dad. We have just asked life a new question; we are no longer asking the same question like we once did' Molly's mum added. 'I get that but I have my own questions to ask too. I know everything is going to be

OK as my intuition says so' Molly said, looking at her mum as she lifted out the locket from under her jumper and began playing with it. 'When did you get so wise?' Molly's mum said, stroking Molly's hair. Molly shrugged her shoulders. 'Is that it? Can I go to the barn now?' Molly asked, getting up from the table.

'There is one more thing' Molly's dad began. 'Would you mind if your mum and I stayed here whilst you visit Yellowstone tomorrow, to sort a few things out' Molly's dad asked tentatively. 'Sure' Molly said dismissively and walked across and pulled on her boots and jacket before heading outside to the barn.

Molly's mum let out a large sigh. 'Of course Nana O knew, that's why she wanted us to go on this trip. It wouldn't surprise me if she didn't already know we would come here and Molly would see Hugh again' Molly's mum said, waving her hands to the sky in frustration. 'Even when she's dead she is still one step ahead!' she exclaimed.

Molly's dad began to laugh at the thought of Nana O sorting everything out from up in the stars. 'Well, all that matters is that Molly understands. She probably understands better than we do' he said, pointing at himself and then at Molly's mum.

Shaking her head in disbelief, Molly's mum stood up and said 'I'm going to go and have a shower.' She got up and made her way to the stairs. As she reached the top and walked along the landing, she heard the front door open followed by a patter of feet.

Molly and Hugh kicked off their boots as they flew in different directions. Ben followed them balancing a pile of logs in his arms as he walked across to the fireplace where he began to build a fire. Ally came in and closed the door behind her as she took off her boots. Molly's dad walked across to join Ben as he watched him build a fire with gladness. Ben struck a match and placed it into the fireplace, watching it burst into light.

'I do love that bit' Ben said, standing back up and looking at Molly's dad. Molly's dad sat down on the couch and watched the flames flicker. 'It sure is a nice spot you have here' he said, looking at Ben. 'I have been very lucky. I am glad to call this home' Ben said, looking up at the ceiling then walking across to the chair next to the couch and sitting down.

Ally walked in with empty glasses and a bottle of wine, and placed them on the coffee table in the centre. Hugh took hold of Molly's hand. 'Follow me' he whispered as he led Molly across the room to the back porch where they slid out the door and quietly closed it behind them.

Hugh walked to the bench and sat down. He stared up at the mountain. Molly walked across to join him. As she followed Hugh's gaze she took out the locket that was hanging around her neck and began to play with it between her fingers.

Hugh saw a glimmer out of the corner of his eyes as he turned to look at Molly. 'What's that?' he asked, pointing to the locket. Molly looked down. 'It was a gift from Nana O' she said distantly. She unclipped it from around her neck and opened it, taking out a small piece of paper from inside. Hugh leaned across and read the words out loud: 'Love is the answer, wishes come true, as you find the place that connects me and you' he said, looking back up at Molly.

'What does that mean?' Hugh said, confused. 'That everything and everyone is connected and we can achieve anything if we follow our intuition. It relates to that passing thought or funny feeling in your stomach when something is going to happen, that asks you to act when you meet certain people or go to certain places, to reach your dreams' Molly said wisely.

'I wear it to remind me to follow my gut feelings when I have asked life a question. It kind of sounds like it complements your vision wall. You focus on what you want and it tells you who you need to speak to in order to get there' Molly said, placing the locket back under her top.

Hugh looked back at the mountain as he considered Molly's words. 'Why do you keep looking at that mountain?' Molly asked, interrupting Hugh's thoughts. Hugh took a deep breath in. 'I'm getting that funny feeling' he said, pointing to his stomach. 'That at the bottom of the mountain is where the next piece of the puzzle is, the next answer to our questions' Hugh said, turning and looking into Molly's eyes.

Molly and Hugh sat quietly as they thought about the adventure they were going to embark on. The door began to open as Molly's mum's head popped out. 'Come on you two, it's time for bed. You have had a busy day today and you'll need to be well rested for tomorrow' she said, gesturing for them to come inside. Molly and Hugh stood up and followed Molly's mum inside.

Hugh walked across to Ally, kissed her goodnight and then headed towards Ben. 'Goodnight, Champion' he said, kissing him goodnight. 'You promise we will go and see him tomorrow?' Hugh asked anxiously. 'Promise' Ben said, smiling. Molly waved goodnight to everyone as she followed Hugh up the stairs and made her way to bed.

4 MIRROR OF MIRACLES

Hugh lay still in his bed as he watched the seconds tick by on his clock, waiting eagerly for morning to arrive. He rolled over and let out a sigh. 'What's taking so long?' he thought, as he stared up at his vision wall. There was a creak as his door slowly began to open. Hugh lifted his head and looked at the bottom of his bed to see Molly's head peering around the door.

'Are you awake?' Molly whispered. 'I can't sleep' he replied, sitting up. 'Me neither' Molly said, navigating her way through Hugh's room and sitting down on his bed. Molly glanced over at the vision wall. 'I wonder what is waiting for us at the bottom of the mountain?' Molly muttered, lost in thought. 'Whatever it is, it's sure to have one result – to make life even more fun! And for us to succeed, so we can receive everything that we wish for' Hugh sat looking at Molly with a cheeky smile.

'What's it like having Ben as your new dad?' Molly asked, secretly feeling upset by what was about to happen in her own life. Hugh looked straight at her, 'It's no better or worse, it's just different. My dad brought one perspective on life and Ben brings a different perspective and I love them both for that' Hugh said. 'Are you sure you're alright about what is happening with your parents?' Hugh asked, concerned.

Molly lifted out the locket and held it in her hand. 'I guess, it stinks, but part of me feels there is something better on its way. I've just got to get there. The atmosphere in the house has been horrible the last couple of months, so at least I won't have that when I go back. I just want to find my home' Molly said, shuffling her feet together as the fear began to rise inside.

Molly looked up quickly, changing the subject. 'So, which one of your pictures is the next to come true?' she asked. Hugh whipped back his duvet and stood up on his bed, pointing to the picture with the words written on it: "world's greatest, champion, number 1". Hugh looked at Molly, beaming. 'It's going to be the best day ever' he said, sitting back down on his bed.

The room started to get lighter as the sun rose up

over the hills. Hugh watched as the room glowed golden. He got down off his bed and went to the bottom of his wardrobe, pulling out a rucksack. He darted around the room and filled it with his camera, jumper and pj's. He sneaked out of his room and into the bathroom, coming back with his toothbrush and placing it in his rucksack. Molly sat hugging her knees as tears started to roll down her cheeks.

Hugh zipped up his bag as he looked over towards Molly. He walked across and sat down next to her, wrapping his arms around her. 'It's ok Molly. It'll be ok, you still have me' Hugh said, hopefully. Molly sniffled. 'How do you know it's going to be ok?' she said, as more tears flowed. 'Because it's only change and that means you can have a say in what that change transforms into' Hugh said, smiling and squeezing Molly tighter. 'But nobody listens to me. I'm invisible!' she cried.

Ben appeared at the door and Hugh looked up pleadingly for Ben to make it all better. Ben sat down next to Molly on the bed and lifted her onto his lap. He wrapped his arms around her and she sat motionless with her head tucked into his neck. 'Molly, you are such an important person in this life. You may just feel like a speck of stardust in this vast universe at the moment but without you the universe would be incomplete. There would be a very important piece missing' Ben said, holding her tight.

Molly looked up and Hugh passed her one of his socks to use as she wiped away her snot. 'I guess' Molly said, looking down at her fingers. Ben leaned back. 'You guess? Well, I know for sure. Life would be incomplete without you, me, Hugh, everyone' Ben said with feeling. 'As we flow down the river of life, there will be times when we have a bumpy ride through the rapids, and it's those times that we have to remember not to bail out on our hopes and dreams but let those rapids make us stronger' Ben said as he kissed Molly on the forehead.

'We all still love you and you'll always have a family. You'll just have a few extra members than most and there will always be a room here for you' Ben said, lifting her onto the bed and standing up. Molly looked up, nodded and began to smile as she started to feel more optimistic. 'Come on, Molly, let's get your stuff ready' Hugh said, climbing off the bed and taking her hand. Ben stepped back out of their way. 'I'll be in the barn getting things ready for Tom's arrival' he said.

Hugh looked back with gratitude. Ben nodded and smiled in acknowledgement before following them out onto the landing. As Ben skipped down the stairs he could hear Hugh whirling around Molly's room. Ben walked into the kitchen as he began to make Ally her morning cup of tea and a fresh pot of coffee.

There was the thunder of feet as Hugh and Molly bounded down the stairs, across the living room and towards the front door. 'We'll come and help you, Ben' Molly said as she slipped on her boots. Hugh opened the front door and there, straight in front of him, were two butterflies sitting on the porch light. 'Ben, Molly, come quick' he whispered, motionless. Ben became curious and walked over, holding Ally's cup of tea. Molly looked up and saw the butterflies too.

The butterflies were pure white. They fluttered their wings momentarily before becoming still again. Ben reached the door and saw them. 'They're an omen aren't they?' Hugh said in awe, turning to look at Ben. 'Hugh, sometimes I think you're on another planet' Molly said, looking confused. 'Some say the butterfly is there to remind us to move through transition and transformation with lightness and playfulness, but I have never seen two together like this before' Ben said, looking down at Hugh and Molly in front of him.

'Oh boy' Ben said in anticipation of what was to come. He turned and headed back towards the stairs. Hugh's smile transformed into a large grin as he bounced up and down in front of Molly. Molly placed her hands on his shoulders, trying to keep his feet on the ground before he floated away with joy.

'Just hold on! What is this all about?' Molly asked, shaking her head. 'Whoop, whoop, yippee!' Hugh yelled as he ran across towards the barn with his arms spread wide like he was a bird flying through the sky. 'Hey, wait for me!' Molly called as she ran behind him. As she reached the barn she saw Hugh scooping out some grain and placing it in buckets. 'So, are you going to tell me what it means?' Molly asked, walking over and picking up one of the buckets. 'I don't need to, Ben already has. Don't you see – the butterflies were for both of us, and they are there to remind us that whatever happens today, we need to be playful and lighthearted about it' Hugh said, breathless. He picked up the buckets and made his way out to the horses.

'That was just a coincidence' Molly said dismissively as they walked to the first gate and placed the buckets inside the pen. Hugh stopped in his tracks. 'Seriously?' he said, looking very unimpressed. 'After all you have learned from the locket and my wall you still think that it's a coincidence?' he said, feeling disappointed as he walked to the next horse and placed a bucket in front of it.

Molly shuffled her feet in the dirt. 'I guess not' she said. Hugh placed the last bucket down and walked back towards Molly. 'You know this – two events coinciding is a coincidence. What are the chances of us ever seeing something like that again?' Hugh continued. 'It doesn't change what is to come but it is there to help us to create the best day we can out of what we have got at the moment' Hugh finished.

Molly stood boldly in front of Hugh. 'The best we have got at the moment!' she erupted. 'Did you not hear what is happening in my life! My whole world is splitting in two!' she yelled, bursting into tears again. 'When are you going to start telling a new story?' Hugh said, shaking his head. 'You see two worlds splitting in two. I see an opportunity to create your own world' he said as he walked by Molly and headed back into the barn.

Molly listened to the horses munching on their grain as she ran her fingers along the silk-like fur. A bubbly feeling began to rise from the pit of her stomach. 'Is he always right?' she muttered in jest to the horse before heading back into the barn. She was greeted by Ben who was emptying sacks of grain. 'He has gone in to get some breakfast before we head off' Ben said as he picked up another sack and began emptying it. Molly nodded as she started to walk past. 'You never know, Molly, your life could transform into something incredible. When you think you have lost everything, that is the moment when you receive what your heart has always wanted' Ben said wisely.

Molly stopped and looked back at Ben. 'Sometimes I think you're just a walking bumper sticker dispenser' she said as she continued to make her way towards the house. Ben began to chuckle. 'Well, that's a new one' he muttered to himself. Molly slowly opened the front door and stepped inside as she looked over to see Ally, Hugh and her parents sitting at the kitchen table.

Ally got up. 'Breakfast is on the table' she said, motioning for Molly to come and join them. Molly slipped off her boots, walked across to the table, sat down and reached for a pancake. Hugh continued to look down as he couldn't hide his disappointment in Molly not believing in the butterflies.

Molly stared at Hugh and then turned to Ally. 'We saw two white butterflies this morning. Ben said they are an omen for transformation' Molly said, proving a point to Hugh. Ally sat back down at the table and picked up her cup of tea. 'When I first arrived I thought that was crazy talk, but now' she paused 'now I believe it to be the truth' she said. 'I think this trip has a gift for all of us' Molly said as she took a mouthful of pancake. 'Maybe I'll transform into a beautiful butterfly' Molly said, looking at Ally. 'Sometimes the butterfly just needs to spread its wings and fly, shining its colours for all to admire' Ally said, winking at Molly.

Hugh sat with his mouth wide open as he couldn't believe what his mom had just said. 'Are you trying to pretend to be a fly catcher?' Ally said jokingly to Hugh. Just then the door opened and Ben walked in. 'Is everything ready to load up as Tom's just arrived?' he said. With perfect timing, Tom stepped through the door. 'Morning, everyone' he said, tipping his hat.

'Morning Tom, coffee?' Ally asked, as she got up and walked towards the coffee machine. Tom sat down next to Hugh before reaching forward and taking some of his pancake. 'Hey!' Hugh protested. Ally looked at Hugh. 'You go and help take the bags to the truck with Ben' Ally instructed as she placed a fresh cup of coffee in front of Tom. 'And you behave yourself' she said, tapping Tom on the shoulder. Hugh slid his chair back and stuck his tongue out at Tom as he went by.

Hugh began dragging the bags across to the front door and Ben then took them down to the truck. 'Looks like you are going to have nice weather for your trip' Tom said as he drank his coffee. 'Yes, thankfully, but we are making a stop on our way to see the man at the bottom of the mountain, whatever that means' Ally said, mystified. Tom blurted out his mouthful of coffee and sprayed everyone.

Ben and Hugh walked back in. Tom shot round and looked at Ben, ready to interrogate. 'So, you are going to the mountain Ally says.' Ben froze. 'I think I left a bag upstairs' he said with a mischievous smile as he suddenly dashed towards the staircase. Tom smirked as he drank the remainder of his coffee. Ally watched them both. 'This is getting more and more suspicious and one of you is going to tell me what the heck is going on or you'll both be sleeping in the barn!' she said, standing up.

Tom stood up too. 'I'll let Ben do the talking, he seems to be good at that' he said. Tom tipped his hat and then made his way towards the front door as Ben reappeared in the living room. Tom pointed towards him. 'When you get back we are doing some roping practice' he announced, before heading out towards the barn.

Ben turned towards everyone – they were still bemused by his actions. 'Ready when you guys are' he said, before turning and heading out to the truck. Ally got up and began to tidy the pots. 'Leave those and get off. I'll do them' Molly's mum said, taking the plates off Ally. 'Are you sure? I don't mind' Ally said. 'Go on, have a great trip' Molly's mum said, motioning for her to head to the door. Ally reached over and gave her a big hug. 'Stay strong' she whispered.

Molly walked across. 'See you when I get back' she said, feeling sad. Molly's mum wrapped her in a hug. 'Have a great time' she said, as she kissed her on the cheek. Molly walked across to her dad and climbed on his lap. 'See you soon' she said, wrapping her arms around his neck. 'In a while, crocodile' he said, hugging her back.

Molly climbed down and walked across to where Ally was waiting. She pulled on her boots and together they headed out towards the truck where Hugh and Ben were waiting. Molly and Ally climbed into the truck. As Ben began to reverse, Molly's parents stood at the front door waving. Molly watched them through the rear window as they drove off down the dirt road.

As they drove along, Molly continued to watch the world pass by out of the rear window. Hugh sat restless in the back seat next to her, eager to get to the mountain. Ben looked across at Ally who was nervously tapping her fingers on her lap. She looked over at Ben. 'You just might as well tell me who we are going to see' she said, frustrated. Ben smiled and looked back at the road. 'I did — the man at the bottom of the mountain' he said, delighted with himself.

Ally slid further down in her seat. Molly turned round to face the front and tried to feel excited. Instead, she felt throbbing pain inside as her life shattering to pieces was too loud. Ben glanced at Molly in the rear view mirror with concern. He reached forward and turned on the radio in an attempt to distract her from her thoughts. Molly looked up at Ben and gave him a weak smile of gratitude.

'Please, life, let him be able to help Molly and Hugh' Ben thought to himself. As the mountain drew rapidly closer and the roads began to bend and twirl around the rolling hills, Ally became engrossed in the breathtaking landscape. 'It's beautiful' Ally said to herself. Ben slowed down the truck as they passed through a small town.

Hugh pressed his face against the window as he watched the stores pass by. Ben looked from side to side as the memories of the past began to emerge from deep inside. Some he wished he could forget. He reached a stop light and turned right, heading back out of the town and into the countryside. As the buildings began to grow smaller, Ben turned left down a small road. Ally pulled herself up and sat bolt upright, her eyes fixed on the small house that lay ahead, overlooked by the mountain.

Ben parked the truck in front of a small log cabin. As he parked up he took a deep breath. 'I really hope he is in a good mood' he thought to himself. Before opening the door and stepping out into the fresh mountain air, Ally sat motionless. The unknown still scared her as she looked around for any signs of life. She watched Ben walk up the steps and knock on the front door.

Ben stood staring at his feet as he shuffled uncomfortably from side to side. 'Why is Ben nervous, mom?' Hugh asked, watching Ben intently. 'Not sure, but it's making me nervous too' Ally said as her heart began to race. Hugh reached for the door handle just as the cabin door opened. There stood a tall, thin man, dressed similarly to Ben but with grey hair and wrinkles etched into his skin.

They both stood for a moment, staring at each other, before the man disappeared back into the house followed by Ben. 'Should we follow them?' Hugh asked impatiently. 'I don't know' Ally said, feeling vulnerable and frozen by her fear. Molly quickly opened the door and ran up the stairs into the house. She couldn't cope with indecisiveness right now. Ally and Hugh soon followed.

They stepped through the front door of the simple log cabin with only the bare essentials: a chair positioned by the fire, a bookshelf in the corner and a dining table. Ally, Hugh and Molly nervously walked through towards the back of the house and reached the kitchen. They looked around for signs of either Ben or the man.

Molly looked around. 'Where are the photos?' she whispered to Hugh, who shrugged in response. Ally reached to take the handle of the back door and it flew open. Ally stepped back just in time. The man screeched to a halt, staring wide-eyed at Ally who glared at him. Ben stepped out from behind. 'Meet my pa' he said, sinking his hands deep into his jean pockets.

'Pa, this is Ally, Hugh and Molly' Ben said tentatively. The man looked them up and down antagonistically, nodded in acknowledgement and stepped around Ally towards the living room. He paused a moment when he reached Molly and Hugh and then continued heading towards his chair. He sat down, placed his elbows on the arm rests and clasped his fingers together.

Ben stepped towards Ally, speechless. 'I'll put the kettle on' Molly said, trying to lighten the atmosphere. Hugh spun round and walked towards the man, bringing one of the dining table chairs and placing it in front of him. The man's focus didn't shift from the floor. 'Hi, I'm Hugh' he said, holding out his hand. The man took in a deep breath. 'Billy' he replied, taking Hugh's hand and shaking it.

Ally glared at Ben. 'A little warning would have been nice' she said. Ben took her hand. 'I wasn't sure if he would be here' Ben said, guiding Ally into the living room and sitting down at the table. Molly started to bring in the cups of tea and a coffee for Ben. 'What do you want, Mr?' Molly said rudely. Billy looked up at her with her hands placed on her hips and grunted 'coffee'.

Molly disappeared back into the kitchen and the room fell silent. Billy looked across to Ben as Molly reappeared with a cup of coffee, handing it to Billy. Billy looked down and noticed the locket around her neck. Molly perched on Hugh's seat and stared intensely at Billy. 'Why don't you have any family photos?' she asked boldly. Ben shuffled nervously in his seat. Billy looked up at Ben. 'Nice to know I've been a big part of your life story' he said sarcastically.

Ben became angry. 'You would have been had you not spent your life as the walking dead the moment grandma and grandpa died' Ben said, standing up and storming out of the back door. Billy went back to staring at his tea. Hugh took the opportunity. 'You have some information for me and Molly' he said, folding his arms across his chest.

'Hugh, not now' Ally said, getting up to find Ben. Hugh watched Ally walk out the back door. When she had disappeared he turned back to Billy. 'Yes, now' he said with authority. 'Yes, what he said' Molly said, folding her arms to mirror Hugh. 'No information here' Billy said, taking a gulp of coffee. 'You're lying' Molly interrupted. 'Your words aren't matching your intention' she said, pointing to his mouth and then his heart.

Billy looked straight into Molly's eyes. 'Where did you get that locket from?' he said hard-heartedly. Molly quickly tucked the locket beneath her top. 'A piece of information for a piece of information' she said, re-folding her arms. Billy began to smile. 'Your persistence will serve you well on your journey' he said, looking at Molly and then at Hugh. 'Most people don't ask or insist enough' he finished. Billy looked towards the back door. 'So, what tales of misery has he told you?' Billy asked, motioning towards where Ben went. 'Actually, he has only just mentioned you in the last couple of days. He wanted you to meet mom for obvious reasons' Hugh said, beginning to relax.

Billy looked back at Hugh. 'Well, I was beginning to think this day wouldn't come' Billy said, getting up and walking across to the bookshelf. He moved one of the books to the side, took out a small box and placed it in his shirt pocket. 'Did you know we were coming?' Molly asked, turning round in her seat towards Billy. 'There had been signs' Billy remarked.

'Now, let's talk about that deal young lady, you have the feistiness of a woman I once knew who had a very similar locket to that' Billy said, as he walked across the living room to a closed door. Molly and Hugh got up and followed Billy as he opened the door and stepped into a dark room.

Billy reached across and turned on the light. Molly and Hugh stepped into the room cautiously. Billy walked over to where a blanket was pinned to the wall, and pulled it down. There hanging on the wall was a mirror with writing inscribed at the top. Molly and Hugh stepped forward and examined the mirror as Billy wiped some dust off with the blanket. Billy then stood back.

'So, what have you learned so far?' Billy asked, staring at Hugh and Molly's reflection in the mirror. Hugh turned round. 'That once you say what you want and focus on it then it will come true. That's how mom and I met Ben' Hugh said. Billy nodded. 'Very good: the law of attraction. And, you, Miss?' Billy said, gazing at Molly. Molly slowly turned round. 'That love connects us all and our intuition is what guides us to the action we need to take to reach our dreams' Molly said quietly.

Billy took a step forward. 'The law of oneness' he said as he placed his hands on Hugh's shoulders and turned him to face the mirror. Molly copied. 'Are you two sure you are ready for the next piece of the puzzle? By now you must know that once you understand, this life will never be the same again. There is no going back to who you were' he said guardedly. 'Yes, absolutely' Hugh said with delight. Billy looked at Molly. Molly looked him straight in the eye and nodded with conviction.

'The person you see is the person you'll be' Billy said, placing his finger on the mirror. Hugh and Molly stared at their reflection. 'The question is — who do you see?' Billy continued. Hugh tilted his head in confusion. 'I see my reflection' he said. Molly stood silently and then began to speak. 'I see a broken girl, lost, feeling homeless and unloved, with nothing going right in her life' she said, as tears began to roll down her cheeks. Hugh looked back at his reflection as he began to understand. 'I see a champion, the world's greatest, the number 1' he said, smiling at his reflection.

'Then that's who you'll be' Billy said, stepping back. 'But I don't want to be that person!' Molly turned round, feeling angry. Billy placed his hands in his jeans pockets and his expression began to soften. 'Well, then change it' he said softly. Molly turned back and faced the mirror. 'But then I would be lying, saying I was something different' she responded. Billy stood behind Molly. 'Your life is only the stage of the role you have been playing' he said. Molly looked at herself again. 'I see hope. I see someone who is loved unconditionally, and who has found her home, where her life is successful in every way, every day' she said.

'Then that is who you'll be' Billy said, pleased. 'Now, don't get caught out because the person you feel right now and the person you see in the mirror will constantly be trying to demand your attention. Just remember, it's your choice who you would like to see. Remind yourself: I believe in that which others may not yet see. Open your heart to be the person you want to be. This is the law of cause and effect' Billy concluded.

'Now, Miss Molly, a piece of information for a piece of information. You should always honour your word. It means you'll be careful choosing the words you speak and the promises you make in the future' Billy said powerfully. Molly turned round and unclasped the locket from around her neck before placing it in Billy's hand. Billy slowly opened it up and saw the piece of paper inside. He quickly closed it and handed it back to Molly.

'Thank you' he said before promptly walking out of the room. Molly ran behind him. Billy sat back down in his chair, resting his elbows on the chair arms and clasping his fingers together. Molly sat down on the chair in front of him and gazed at him. Then she suddenly remembered. 'Oh my! You're him!' she exclaimed. Billy didn't move. 'You are the man from the photo of Nana O, on one of her adventures!' she continued to yell.

Hugh quickly ran into the room to see an elated Molly. Billy continued to sit silently as Molly looked down at the locket in her hand. 'Maybe you need this more than me' she said, holding it out towards Billy. Billy looked down at the locket and then slowly folded Molly's fingers back around it. 'Just seeing it is enough for me to get the message. Your Nana O was very good at saying clearly what she meant in very few words' he said as his eyes sparkled with life at the memory.

'Keep hold of it. Let it continue to remind you of the truths you have already learned on this journey' Billy said as he began to glow with joy. Molly re-attached the locket around her neck. 'I promise' she said, leaning across and hugging Billy.

They heard the back door begin to open. Molly sat

back up and was joined by Hugh who then gave Billy a hug. 'Thank you, now I understand how I can reach my dreams' Hugh said. Ben appeared at the door of the kitchen. 'We need to be making a move you two' Ben said, looking longingly at Hugh and Molly. 'Did you find what you were looking for?' Ben asked. Calmly, they both nodded before standing up from the chair.

'I hope we will see you again' Hugh said, looking at Billy. 'All you need to do is ask' Billy said quietly. Hugh took the chair and placed it back by the table and then walked with Molly out of the front door. Ally walked into the living room. 'Well, nice to meet you' she said coldly, holding her hand out towards Billy. Billy rose from his chair, walked across and took Ally's hand. 'You sure are a miracle, Miss Ally' Billy said gladly. 'Sorry about the rude introduction, it's just you were a bit of a surprise. I had lost hope that this day would come' he finished.

Ally looked at him confused. 'I'll leave that story for Ben to tell some day. Now, if you wouldn't mind I would like a moment alone with my son' Billy said. Ally slowly began to make her way to the front door. As she looked behind Ben smiled sweetly and nodded that it was ok. Ally stepped outside and headed towards the truck where Molly and Hugh were waiting.

Billy stepped towards Ben. He reached inside his

pocket and took out the small box. He took hold of Ben's hand and placed it in his palm. 'I hope you have as much eternal happiness, love and luck as your grandma and grandpa did' Billy said. Tears began to form in Ben's eyes. 'I wish ...' he choked before stopping himself. Billy stepped forward and hugged Ben. 'Me too, but they have got the best view of all, I'm sure they are happy we have seen each other again' Billy said tearfully.

Ben was just about to speak but Billy held up his hand to stop him. 'Let's not let our past be the story of our future' he said. Ben nodded. 'I'd best get going' he said, pointing to the front door. Billy nodded in agreement. 'Have a safe journey, son' he said. Ben smiled, placed the box in his jeans pocket and made his way out the front door. Ben skipped down the steps and hopped into the truck before turning on the ignition. The three in the truck all wondered at his sudden change in mood. 'Right, Yellowstone here we come' Ben said happily as he turned the truck around and began to drive back down the road.

5 BACK TO TRUTH

As they drove down the road in silence, Molly and Hugh looked at each other in bewilderment as they listened to Ben humming along to the radio. Ally looked across, frowning. 'OK, you, it really is time to spill the beans. What is going on or am I getting out of this truck right now?!' Ally threatened. Ben smiled softly. 'I wouldn't recommend that, I'd miss you too much' is all he said as he reached across and took Ally's hand, placing it in his.

'No, that is just not good enough anymore. Talk!' Ally said more firmly, taking her hand out of his. 'It's a surprise. Actually, it isn't really, it's just perfect timing. That moment when the veil between your dreams and reality lifts and it's just a matter of waiting to live the moment' Ben said, taking back her hand.

'What dream is about to come true?' Molly called

from behind. Hugh quickly nudged her with his elbow and shook his head, motioning for her to stay quiet. Ben looked in the rear view mirror and winked at Molly. 'See, that's what I'm talking about. How can I trust you when you are obviously keeping something from me' Ally said, throwing her hands up in the air in frustration.

'Wow, you really hate surprises' Ben said, glancing across at Ally. 'If you have forgotten the last surprise I received it was losing Hugh's dad!' Ally said beginning to cry. Ben sat quietly shaking his head. 'No, the last surprise you had was meeting me' Ben said confidently. 'You can keep being the person who lost someone you loved or you can be the person who has found a new love' Ben said, emphasising his point.

Ally didn't look up but turned to look out of the car window. 'Maybe' Ally said quietly. 'But how long is this one going to last?' Ally asked herself. 'As long as it is meant to but I'm grateful for all the moments we have together, rather than thinking about the moments we spend apart' Ben said, squeezing Ally's hand.

Hugh leaned forward and placed his hand on Ally's shoulder. 'Mom, it's ok to be someone new, I won't love you any less. I haven't forgotten him but I haven't stop living either. If anything, I live more as I make a point of seeing the detail in each day. I think dad would have been proud of us and what we have achieved' Hugh said encouragingly. 'Your grandma doesn't think so. I didn't know you could fit reckless into one sentence so many times' Ally responded, as the thought annoyed her as she remembered her last phone call.

Hugh sat back in his seat. 'Oh, Ally, you're so reckless' he said, imitating his grandma's voice. Ally began to chuckle. 'How could you do this Ally? What kind of a woman are you?' he continued, as Hugh placed his hands on his hips. Ally's chuckles transformed into a roaring laughter which echoed around the truck.

Molly smiled. 'Well, that woman scares me' she added, causing Ally and Hugh to laugh even louder. Ben pretended to pull a worried face at Molly. 'Maybe I'll be away that day she comes to the ranch' Ben said, as they too began to laugh. Molly interrupted. 'Look! Look!' she said, leaning forward and pointing out of the window as the truck rolled by the sign saying "Yellowstone National Park".

Ben became more serious as he watched the signs passing by. They took a left and followed the road as it began to bend and wind through the landscape. All the way to the horizon were rolling hills and mountains. Hugh and Molly watched the bison eating in the lowland as deer leaped across the road and the clouds cascaded shadows over the hills. Everyone fell quiet in awe at the wonder of nature and the peace, harmony and unity of such strength in the stillness that surrounded them.

Ben started to slow down and Ally sat up in her seat. 'Is everything ok?' she asked, looking at him worriedly. Ben pulled the car to a stop and motioned for them all to come closer as he pointed out ahead of them to a nearby ridge. Ally's hands flew to her mouth as she gasped. They all watched intently as a bear and two cubs made their way along slowly and gracefully walking into some nearby trees.

The truck remained silent as Ben pulled off and continued down the road. Hugh and Molly slid back in their seats, speechless. Ally slowly lowered her hands and took hold of Ben's, looking across at him with pure gratitude. 'I should have trusted you more' Ally whispered. As they looked ahead they saw a cluster of cabins and Hugh began to bounce in his seat. 'Aden!' he cried with excitement.

Molly became uncomfortable again as she took out her locket and began to play with it. Ben squinted. 'Sally and John have already arrived. I can see their truck' Ben said as he began to accelerate. Hugh's eyes focused on the truck parked up ahead as they drew closer. As they reached the cabins, Ben swung his truck round and parked it next to John's.

Suddenly, Aden appeared at Molly's side of the door

which caused her to scream with fright. 'Hugh!' Aden called and disappeared round the other side of the truck. Hugh leaped out of the truck and hugged Aden. 'You'll never believe what we have seen' Hugh said, bursting with excitement. 'Wait until you see the river' Aden responded, pulling Hugh up towards the front door of the cabin as Sally and John were stepping out. 'Hey you!' John said, as Hugh and Aden whizzed by and disappeared inside.

Ally stepped out of the truck as Sally bounded down towards her to embrace her in a hug. Ben turned around in his seat to look at Molly. 'Are you ok to meet everyone?' he asked cautiously. Molly took in a deep breath. 'I just don't want to be the broken kid' Molly said distantly. 'Well, you heard what Billy said — it's up to you to show the world the person you want to be and I won't tell them if that isn't who you are' Ben said, before opening his door, stepping out and walking across to shake John's hand.

Molly hesitated as she reached for the door. 'I'm ok, I'm ok' Molly started to repeat to herself as she stepped out and walked across to where the adults were standing. As Molly walked to Ally's side, Ally reached across and placed her arm on Molly's shoulder and pulled her into her side. 'And this is magical Molly. She is the daughter of my friends from England and has come to stay with us for a little while' Ally said, winking at Molly.

'Well, magical Molly, pleased to meet you' Sally said, wrapping her in a hug. Molly looked across to John. 'Hello, Molly' he said politely. 'We have only just arrived' Sally said, stepping back and hinting at John. 'I guess that's my cue to bring in the rest of the bags. You be careful, Ben, they train you without you knowing' John said jokingly as he scooted by Sally so he was just out of reach of her hand swinging through the air.

'Well, that's you and me both buddy' Ben said, following in John's footsteps. 'They say it like it's a bad thing' Sally said playfully to Molly. 'Come on, let's go inside' she said. Ally kept her arm around Molly as they walked into the cabin. In the centre of the living room there was an open stone fire surrounded by leather couches and a bookshelf. There were some patio door opening out onto a large decking area with a stunning view of the land and a river flowing through.

Sally and Ally walked into the kitchen as Sally began to unpack the food. 'Is a BBQ tonight alright?' Sally asked, as she stuck her head in the fridge. 'Perfect' Ally responded as she started to fill the kettle up. She watched Hugh and Aden sprint up towards the patio doors and into the living room. 'Mom!' he called. 'In here' Ally replied, as Hugh and Aden followed her voice into the kitchen. 'Aden, this is Molly. She is from England too' Hugh said. 'Hi, I'm Aden' he said, shuffling shyly from side to side. 'Hi' Molly responded as she wondered why he had become so shy. Sally turned round with her arms full of food and nearly tripped over Aden as she stumbled and fell into the fridge door. 'Right, you three go and entertain yourself for a while whilst we unpack' Sally said in frustration, whilst rebalancing the food in her hands.

The three of them backed out of the kitchen slowly and then, when reaching the living room, sprinted back outside across the decking out into the wilderness. Sally smirked across to Ally. 'I haven't lost my touch' she said. John and Ben appeared at the doorway. 'Oh, yes please' John's eyes widened with delight as he watched Ally making a cup of tea. 'He has been so excited to have one of your cups of tea, Ally. It's all he has talked about for the last few days' Sally said, shaking her head.

Ally passed him a cup as John took a long sip. 'Oh how I have missed you' he said longingly, giving Ally a hug. Ally chuckled. 'We'll go and sort out the grill and some firewood for later' John said, nursing his tea with joy as he and Ben made their way outside. Sally and Ally pulled up two chairs and faced them out towards the incredible view. They watched Hugh, Molly and Aden making their way down the path towards the river that was flowing by.

Hugh and Aden walked quickly and continued to follow the path down as the noise of the river began to grow. Molly kept some distance between herself and the boys as she watched them power walk forward. Aden stopped and turned around, noticing Molly way behind them and slowed down as he waited for her.

Molly began to feel relief as she quickened her pace to join Aden. As she reached him, Aden stepped to the side to let Molly pass, and then continued to walk following her. 'So, when did you arrive?' Aden asked sweetly as he watched Hugh disappear down onto the pebbles lining the river. 'A couple of days ago. It was a bit of a spur of the moment adventure that Nana O sent us on' Molly replied, smiling with glee. As the path widened, Aden stepped up and walked alongside Molly.

'I wish I was as confident as him' Aden said, pointing to Hugh who was sitting down. Molly looked across. 'Confidence isn't always about being the loudest. It's more about believing in yourself, especially when the world isn't seeing what you see yet' Molly said encouragingly. As they approached Hugh they sat down on either side of him.

Hugh picked up a pebble and threw it into the river. Aden looked across at Hugh. 'So mate, what's new?' Aden asked as he watched Hugh in deep thought. 'Everything and anything' Hugh said vaguely. Molly leaned forward and looked across to Aden. 'We have got another piece to the puzzle' she said. Aden looked back confused. 'You remember my vision wall and how it taught me about the law of attraction?' Hugh began. 'Yes, of course, actually, because of that we've got one too' Aden said, smiling at the thought.

'Well, I had the next piece about the law of oneness' Molly said, lifting out her locket and dangling it in front of Aden. She opened it up, took out the piece of paper and handed it to Aden. 'Love is the answer, wishes come true, as you find the place that connects me and you' Aden read aloud. He looked up at Molly. 'It means that we are all connected in some way and it's our intuition that guides us to the opportunities and people to help those dreams come true. That's if we follow it, most people are too busy or afraid to' Molly explained.

'What's intuition?' Aden asked, still confused. 'You know, that funny bubbly feeling in your stomach about a thought of something you should do or a dream that is actually trying to guide you, stuff like that' Molly said, as she watched Aden's expression begin to soften. 'Yeah, I know exactly what you mean, not that I act on it' he said, looking down at his feet.

'Well, we met Ben's dad this morning and he showed us this mirror and said the person you see staring back at you in the mirror is who you'll be' Hugh said as he pondered the thought. 'The person you see is the person you'll be. The law of cause and effect' Molly butted in. 'I don't see what the problem is?'

Aden said calmly. Hugh stood up. 'It's one thing to know it but how am I supposed to use it to help me be a champion?' he said, as he kicked another stone.

'Did Billy not say anything else?' Aden asked, standing up too. Hugh just shook his head. Aden picked up and threw a stick and watched it drift down the river as the current carried it along.

'That's it!' Aden shouted, pointing to the stick. Molly got up to see what Aden was pointing to. Hugh looked at him with scepticism. 'You're going to have to explain' he said. 'Well…' Aden said, picking up another stick and throwing it in the water, '…look, watch the stick. You're expecting it to flow down the river. You don't even expect it to get stuck. All you can see is the stick flowing with the river downstream to wherever it is meant to go. Well, imagine you're the stick and life is the river. Maybe what Billy was talking about was seeing the way it is going to be, like the stick successfully flowing down the river' Aden said, delighted.

Molly bit her lip. 'But what I thought he meant was that you are meant to feel all the feelings that person you want to be would feel during the day' she said as Aden looked at her. 'I guess it could be that too' he said. 'I thought what Billy meant was that you're supposed to think like the person you are meant to be, like I am already a champion, I have already succeeded' Hugh said, as he glanced at Molly and then at Aden.

'Well, we are none the wiser' Aden said, sitting back down. Molly slid off her shoes, walked to the water's edge and let the crystal clear water glide over her feet. Her mind began to settle watching the water flow by. 'Why don't we try all of them?' Molly said, looking behind her at Hugh and Aden. 'You' as she pointed to Hugh 'think about the person you want to be, a champion, and you' Molly said, then pointing to Aden 'erm, what is that you want?' Molly asked realising that she didn't know about his dreams. Aden thought for a moment. 'To be confident, but the confident you described. Believing in myself and what I have learned, sharing that with everyone' Aden said, contemplating his words. 'OK, so practise seeing that and I'll feel the person I want to be and how she will handle each moment of the day. Whoever reaches their goal first means that's the way it should be' Molly said as she started to walk a bit further into the water, watching it rise up her legs.

'Sounds good to me' Hugh said excitedly. He looked round at Aden who nodded in agreement. Hugh looked up and saw Ben and John making their way towards them. He turned back to look at Molly who was already deeper into the water. As she took another step, enjoying the feeling of the water pushing against her legs, she placed her foot down and squealed as something sharp pricked her foot.

She quickly lifted her foot out of the water which caused her to lose her balance. She fell back into the water and the current swept her body away as she began to flow down the river. 'Help!' Molly cried as her screams began to fill the air. Hugh froze as he watched Molly's head disappear under the water. Molly's head re-emerged briefly as she gasped for air.

As John and Ben heard Molly's screams, they ran quickly towards the river. Ben ran past Hugh, down the pebbles lining the river's edge to get in line with Molly. He looked up and saw a tree low enough for Molly to grab. 'Molly, grab the branch!' Ben shouted in desperation. Molly's head disappeared back under the water and as she re-emerged again she gasped again for breath. 'Molly, grab the branch!' Ben shouted louder.

Molly looked across to where Ben was pointing. 'Hugh, go and grab my ropes from the back of the truck' Ben shouted urgently. Hugh sprinted back towards the cabin. 'Come on, Molly, you can do this' Ben whispered desperately under his breath. Molly felt the water twisting and twirling her body around like a leaf in the middle of a hurricane.

As she fought to keep her head above water she saw out of the corner of her eye a white feather drift gently down and land gracefully on the water. 'Come on, Molly, you can do this' Molly said, suddenly feeling a surge of strength rise up from inside. Molly started to move and kick towards the rapidly approaching branch.

Hugh reappeared with Ally and Sally following behind. John grabbed the ropes from Hugh's hand and ran towards Ben, as Ben continued to follow Molly down the river. Molly's eyes fixed on the branch, which was only a moment away. 'Yes, I can do this' Molly said as she launched herself towards the branch. She felt the bark between her fingers as she let out a sigh of relief.

'Keep going, Molly, you need to pull yourself up!' Ben watched, fixated. Molly looked across at him. 'OK, 3, 2, 1' Molly heaved herself up as she flopped over the branch with exhaustion. Molly heard cheers faintly in the background from everyone. 'Thank you' Molly muttered to herself as she stared down into the water and watched the white feather drift under the branch and continue down the river.

Molly heard the sound of splashing. As she lifted up her head she saw Ben wading across the river, pulling a rope behind him. 'Well, how was your swimming lesson?' Ben said, smiling. He reached Molly and tied the rope around the tree. 'OK, you can tie it' Ben called back to John, as he watched him tie the other end around a tree nearby.

'OK young lady, time to get back on dry land' Ben said, helping Molly back into the water. 'I want you to hold on to the rope tight, OK, I'll be here with you every step of the way' he said. Molly cautiously took hold of the rope. 'Are you sure it'll hold?' she quivered. Ben pretended to be offended. 'Do you not trust my rope skills?' he enquired sarcastically. Molly smiled. 'Well, I didn't want to say anything' she reciprocated. She took her first step and clutched onto the rope, causing her knuckles to go white. She felt the current begin to get stronger and push against her legs. 'You're doing great' Ben said, as he followed closely behind.

Molly took another step forward and placed her foot down. A rock beneath moved and caused her to wobble. Ben quickly put his arm around her waist. 'I've got you, but you're going to have to do this for yourself' he said, as he watched Molly's eyes begin to fill with tears of fear. 'You're stronger than you realise' he said, taking his arm away.

Molly stared for a moment at Ben. 'You're right' she said as she turned back and focused on where John was standing. She took another step more confidently, pulling on the rope as her steps quickened. 'Nearly there' Molly muttered to herself. 'Keep going, Molly' Aden shouted.

Molly felt the water begin to get lower and lower as she stepped onto the pebbles and out of the water.

'Yes!' Molly said, looking up at the sky. 'Great job' Ben said, putting his arm around Molly's shoulder as they made their way back towards where Sally, Aden, Hugh and Ally stood. Ally bent down and wrapped Molly in her arms. 'You were incredible!' she whispered. Ally stood back up and she and Ben walked either side of Molly. They made their way back up the path towards the cabin.

John looked across at Sally who sighed with relief. 'You worry too much' he said before following Ally. 'Well, someone has to do the worrying around here' Sally replied, insulted. Aden walked past. 'No, that job can stay vacant' he murmured. Sally looked surprise and followed in silence. Hugh looked down the river once more. 'Who would think the river is so strong, yet on the surface it looks so still?' Hugh said to himself, as he turned to follow everyone back to the cabin whilst looking at the wildflowers that lined the path.

'You'd better get a shower and put on some dry clothes' Ally said as they entered the cabin. 'I'll make a start on the BBQ' Ben said, before turning and heading back outside again. 'And I need tea!' Ally announced to herself as she walked into the kitchen.

She looked out the window to see everyone taking a seat on the decking as Ben started heating up the BBQ. Molly reappeared at the kitchen doorway, still dripping with water. 'Is everything OK?' Ally asked, alarmed. Molly couldn't hold back the tears anymore. Ally rushed across and kneeled to hug her. 'It's ok, it's all over now, you made it' she reassured Molly. As Molly snuffled, she lifted her head off Ally's shoulder to say 'they are not...' she took in another breath '...sad tears' Molly stuttered. Ally looked at her, feeling confused. 'I just surrender to it all' Molly said as more tears fell. 'To it all, I just surrender' she finished. As she flopped her head on Ally's shoulder, Ally began to rock her from side to side. 'Well, you have achieved something most don't even realise. Nana O would be so proud of you: to relinquish the control and trust in life is something extraordinary, Molly. Maybe I got it wrong: you're Miracle Molly, when the impossible happens anyway' Ally said, amazed.

Molly took a step back, smiled silently and headed back towards the bathroom. Ally paused for a moment as she stared blankly out into the living room, lost in thought. Ally stood up and looked up at the kitchen ceiling as she took in a deep breath. 'I too surrender all that I am to love, you know what I desire, and I trust you will get me there, I will do what you ask of me' she whispered. Ally felt her body begin to lighten and her mind become clear.

She took hold of her cup of tea and walked out onto the decking. Ben glanced across at Ally and looked at her knowingly. 'You look different' he commented, as

Ally glowed. Ally smiled wisely. 'I think I'm starting to get it' Ally replied, as she walked across and sat down next to Sally.

'I'll go and get the meat and another beer' John said as he reached for his empty bottle. Sally looked across at Ben and then at Ally. 'I'll make a start on the salad. Boys, you can help me' Sally said, standing up and motioning for them to do the same. Ben continued to stare down at the empty grill, listening to everyone leaving behind him.

Aden and Hugh got up quickly and made their way inside, followed by Sally as she patted Ben on the shoulder as she walked by. Ben looked up and smiled. Ally watched everyone vanish as her gaze drifted across to the rolling hills where the sun was beginning to disappear, causing the sapphire sky to turn ablaze with orange and red streaks.

Ben tucked his hand in his jeans pocket and turned around, casually making his way across to Ally. As he crouched down in front of her, Ally continued to watch the sunset transform. 'Have you ever seen anything so beautiful?' Ally said gratefully. 'Nope. It's the best view I have ever had' Ben replied, continuing to look at Ally. Ally looked across to Ben. 'Ha ha, very funny' she said, tapping the brim of his hat. Ben reached across, took hold of Ally's tea and placed it on the floor. He took her hands in his. 'Ally, there is something I was wondering?' Ben began. 'Arrgghh!'

suddenly Molly came running out onto the decking as Hugh chased her with a fish's head. 'Hugh get it away from me!' Molly yelled as she ran across and climbed onto Ally's lap.

'Monkey! Enough!' Ally commanded as she let go of Ben's hands to hold Molly. Ben bowed his head and stood back up. He walked across into the cabin. John passed him at the door as he went outside. 'What's up with him?' John looked across to Ally. Ally shrugged her shoulders. 'I have been asking the same question' she said.

John walked across to the BBQ and placed the meat and fish on the grill. 'So, how are things with you?' Ally asked as Molly scooted off her knee and sat down on the chair next to her. 'Same old in some ways. But then again life hasn't been the same since we met you and Hugh. Something inside was ignited' John said, taking a seat. Sally appeared. 'Ignited? Don't you mean that meeting Ally and Hugh was like putting petrol onto a smouldering fire?' Sally said as she pointed to Ally.

'We have never dreamed so big, made so much progress and never been happier. You inspired us, Ally, and woke us up from a slumber we didn't even realise we had been taking. I guess you kind of get comfortable and then stop living' Sally said, slightly disturbed by her words. 'Don't thank me, it was Hugh. And I would add Molly as well. I have a feeling she'll be having a similar effect on all of us' Ally said, looking across with pride. 'Not just me but Aden too, we are in this together as a trio' Molly added.

'A triangle' a voice said as Ben stepped out of the cabin and onto the decking to join them. Molly leaned forward, resting her head on her hands, listening intently for Ben to continue. 'You three are the triangle' Ben said. Hugh and Aden bounced outside, felt the atmosphere and quickly sat down on the nearest chairs. 'No matter which side of the triangle you put pressure on, it will never break. It is a sign of resilience. When the triangle is pointing up...' Ben said, pointing to Hugh and Aden '...it is about masculinity and aspiration, however, when the triangle is pointing down...' Ben moved his hand across to point at Molly '...it is feminine and about divinity. Yet, combine those together, not only do we have the triangle...' as Ben pointed to all three of them '...together you mirror each other and create the diamond: the symbol of clarity and wisdom, not only of what is above and below but also the four corners, mastery of the four elements.' Ben paused a moment as silence filled the air.

'This is no coincidence. Your three paths crossed and keep crossing each time you find out a new truth about life. A journey is meant to be taken together, unified' Ben sat back in his chair as he looked up at the darkening sky.

Everyone remained quiet as they thought about what they had just heard. John lifted up his bottle in the air. 'Well, if that's the case, cheers! To the adventures taken and the adventures yet to come' he said. Ben reached across and chinked his bottle with John's.

'Oh, boy' Sally said, shaking her head. 'So what you mean is that we have a lot more of this to come' Sally said, pointing back down the path. Ben raised his eyebrows at Sally. 'Well, in that case I shall organise a regular truckload of tea to be delivered' Ally said, chuckling as she reached down and picked up her tea. Molly looked across to Hugh and Aden, and smiled with excitement. Hugh leaned back and put his hands behind his head, smiling back at her in agreement.

'Well, even if you are our wisdom warriors you still need to help set the table' Sally said, waving her hands for the three of them to go and bring out the plates, cutlery and salad. 'One team, one dream' Hugh chimed as he stood up and placed his hand in the centre. Aden stood up and put his hand on top of Hugh's. Molly chuckled and stood to place her hand on top of Aden's. They then made their way inside.

Ben looked back up at the clear sky as the stars began to shine with hope. Molly came back out with the plates, Hugh followed behind with the bowl of salad and Aden came out carrying the cutlery. 'Thank you, monkey' Ally said, as Hugh placed the bowl in the centre of the table and sat back down.

Ben took one of the plates and placed the meat and fish from the BBQ on it before joining everyone at the table and placing the plate in the centre. 'Well, we'd better get fuelled up ready for our walk about tomorrow' John said, reaching across and taking a piece of steak. 'Where are we going?' Aden asked. 'There are a few trails around that should take us a couple of hours' John said as he took a bite. 'Then come back here for some lunch and maybe do some fishing if we have chance, before heading off again' John finished. Hugh reached across and took another piece of chicken. 'Sounds good to me' he said, as they continued to finish off the rest of the food.

John leaned back in his chair and patted his stomach. 'Well, that was a feast fit for a king' he said, satisfied. 'Maybe those trails will do you good' Sally said, looking towards his stomach. 'It's all paid for' John replied, ignoring her.

Molly stood up and began to collect the plates. She was soon joined by Ben as they made their way together into the cabin and put the plates down on the kitchen side. Molly walked across to the sink and began to fill it with water. As Ben reached for the towel, Molly picked up the first plate, swishing it around in the bubbles and wiping it clean before handing it to Ben.

Ben took hold of it. 'Are you alright about what happened today, Molly?' Ben asked. Molly stayed quiet for a moment as she thought, then passed him the next plate. 'I thought I was going to die but then I saw the white feather and it kind of felt like a sign from Nana O. Then I felt this sudden strength inside to keep going' Molly said, looking across to Ben. Ben just nodded for her to continue. 'But when I got on the branch it was like every part of me surrendered to it all and I felt so peaceful' Molly finished, taking the next plate.

'Well, Molly, sometimes we need to let go but sometimes we need to surrender to what we want and get out of the way so life can take its natural course. Most of the time when life takes the reins and we listen, things normally work out better than we could ever have imagined' Ben said, taking the next plate off Molly.

'Is that what you were doing when you looked up at the stars?' Molly asked. Ben looked down shyly and smiled. 'Yes, I been trying to figure out how to do something for a while by organising every single moment. However, every time I do it's like I get in my own way and trip over my own feet, so I have handed it over to life to organise it for me. Life knows what I want but how I get there is up to life. I just need to listen to that and then act when it feels right' Ben said, pointing to Molly's locket.

Molly walked across to dry her hands on the towel. 'I think I'm just going to head to bed, it's been a long day' Molly said. Ben put down the towel and wrapped Molly in a bear hug. 'Sweet dreams, Miracle Molly' whispered Ben. 'Thank you for everything, Ben' Molly said softly, as she stood back and disappeared off towards her room.

Ben walked out onto the decking. 'Where's Molly?' Aden asked. 'She has gone to bed – it's been a big day for her' replied Ben. 'I think that's a sensible idea' Ally conjectured, looking across to Hugh. 'Oh, but…' he groaned. Ally rose her hand to stop Hugh. 'You'll need all your energy for tomorrow' she retorted. Hugh sluggishly got up out of his chair. Sally looked across to Aden. Aden stood up too. 'Night everyone', 'Night boys' John and Ben replied. Hugh and Aden made their way back inside and to their rooms.

6 BUILDING BRIDGES

As Molly lay in bed she tossed from side to side. Each time she closed her eyes she felt like she was back in the river, her body being swept away by the water, gasping for air. Molly shot open her eyes once more as the fear raged inside. She moved her pillow to the end of the bed where she could lay looking out of the window. Molly watched the moon move across the night sky. Her mind became stiller as the stars speckled the sky. 'Somewhere up there, Nana O is probably off on her own adventures' Molly thought to herself.

Molly became even more uncomfortable as she started to realise that she was losing everyone that ever meant anything to her. 'No more Nana O, no more mum and dad. Do I have to decide who I want to live with? What if I don't want to live with either of them? Nana O, I'm so confused and lost, help me find my way back home' Molly whispered.

Molly continued to stare at the moon illuminating the night sky. As her mind became silent she took in a breath and felt the air fill her lungs as she let out a sigh. Molly's gaze drifted around the room and, as she scanned, she saw the single wooden chair in the corner with her clothes draped over, then a chest of drawers with a mirror resting on top.

Molly sat up and looked at the mirror. 'Well, I guess there is no time like now' she said, as she walked towards the mirror. She lifted it off the chest of drawers and placed it on the ground, leaning it up against the wall. Molly sat down, crossed her legs and stared into the mirror. As she looked at her reflection she began to frown. 'Maybe this isn't going to be as easy as I first thought' she said as she continued to scowl at herself.

Molly looked away, placing her head on her hand which rested on her leg. 'But I don't like what I see' Molly said to the night sky. She glanced back at her reflection out of the corner of her eye as the feelings of desperation began to take over. 'I really don't see how this is going to help, come on Molly get a grip of your thoughts' Molly readjusted herself in front of the mirror.

'Miracle Molly, how would she see herself' Molly said,

as her face changed to a look of confusion.
'Confused? Angry?...' as she made an angry face
'...Sad?' as she pretended to wipe away a tear.
'Funny?' as she stuck her tongue out and began to
smile at herself. 'Yes, that's it, smiley!' as Molly sat
smiling to herself. She started to feel her shoulders
relax as she rested a hand on each knee. 'Strong, too'
she said, looking at herself sitting tall.

Molly closed her eyes. 'What would home feel like?'
she asked, as a warmth of excitement flowed round
her body making her smile even more. Molly opened
her eyes slowly and saw herself beaming with
happiness. 'Positive, that anything is possible, I just
need to be patient until it does, but being persistent
each day to reach it' Molly said to herself.

Molly closed her eyes again as she focused on the
excited feeling that was still growing stronger inside
of home. Molly started to chuckle, then opened her
eyes as she bounced around the floor. Molly could no
longer sit still anymore, feeling so thrilled about the
thought of home. 'Yes!' she yelled, waving her arms in
the air. She then flung her hands to her mouth as she
remembered everyone else was asleep and continued
to try and smother her giggles of joy.

Molly looked back at herself in the mirror and didn't
recognise the person who was now staring back at
her. 'Is it really that easy to feel so good?' she said to
herself. She looked straight into her own eyes as they

sparkled. 'Of course it is' she said to herself
confidently. Molly stood back up and walked across
to her bed, climbed back in, pulled the duvet up to
her chin and looked out of the window.

Where the moon was beginning to disappear out of
sight, Molly let her eyes slowly close, still smiling to
herself, as sleep slowly crept in. Molly awoke to a
thud, followed by another thud on her bed as she
sleepily opened her eyes to find Hugh and Aden
sitting there. Molly wearily rubbed her eyes. 'Morning,
lads' she said croakily, as she propped herself up. 'So,
what was last night about?' Hugh asked eagerly.

Molly let out a yawn. 'What do you mean?' she said,
bewildered. 'We heard you yelling last night' Hugh
said impatiently. Molly began to smile again as she
remembered how she had felt when she was in front
of the mirror. Molly sprang out of bed and went to sit
back down in front of the mirror, crossing her legs.
Molly turned back around. 'Well, come on' she said to
Hugh and Aden. Aden and Hugh climbed off the
bed, walked across the room and sat either side of
Molly.

Molly sat up and began to smile, placing her hands on
her knees. She slowly closed her eyes as she searched
inside for that feeling of home. Hugh and Aden
watched as she scowled, then frowned. 'I don't get it'
Molly said, as her eyes shot open. 'I can't find it' she
said, frustrated. 'Last night I did this and I found the

feeling of home and it felt so amazing, there was so much love and happiness that I couldn't keep it in, that's why I screamed as I was so excited' Molly looked back at her reflection. 'But I can't seem to find it now' she finished.

Aden placed his hand on Molly's shoulder. 'The fact that you know what you're looking for means you're halfway there' he said. Molly smiled gratefully at Aden. 'I guess so, I just need to practise' she replied.

Sally peered round the door as she stared at the three of them sitting with crossed legs on the floor. 'I won't ask' she said, shaking her head. 'Breakfast is on the table' she announced, before exiting and heading to the decking. Hugh and Aden got up and followed Sally. Molly watched them leave the room. She turned back to the mirror and began to smile at herself. She moved her finger so it was touching the mirror as she watched her reflection touch back. 'I'm not going to give up on you, ever' she said with conviction to herself.

Molly stood up and lifted her clothes that were draped over the back of the chair. She took off her pj's and pulled on her clothes, before heading out towards the decking area to find everyone sitting around the table. Molly walked across to sit next to Ben. 'Morning, Miss Molly' Ben said, smiling across to her as he reached and placed some bacon on the plate in front of her. 'Morning' Molly said as she took some bread and made herself a bacon sandwich.

'What do you think about this route?' John said, placing the map down on the table and pointing to a line on the map as he looked at Ben. 'John, please can't it wait until after breakfast?' Sally said, cross as she lifted the corner of the map out of her coffee. John lifted the map back up, smirking to himself. 'Of course, love' he said mockingly. Sally glared back at him. 'We'll do well not to get lost. I think Ben should be in charge of the map' she retorted.

'Spoilsport! Where is your sense of adventure?' John asked, pushing his chair back from the table and placing the map down on his knees. 'Like I was saying…' he said, motioning for Ben to look. Ben glanced down and then looked up across the landscape. 'Yeah, I think that'll be good. It should only take us a few hours hiking' he said. Sally stood up from the table. '*Should* being the key word in that sentence' she remarked, as she looked across towards John before heading inside to fetch some more bacon.

Sally reappeared with another plate of bacon and placed it in the centre of the table. Multiple hands reached in to take a piece and the plate became empty again. 'Well, eat up everyone. We head out in thirty minutes!' John said, getting up from the table holding the map. 'Yes, captain' Aden said as he saluted, before taking a large bite of his bacon sandwich. Sally sat back down and took hold of her coffee as she leaned back in her chair. 'We are on holiday, there is no rush' she said, as she took a sip. John looked at Sally and raised his eyebrow before disappearing inside. Ally looked across at Sally. 'Maybe we should just let the men take the kids and we'll stay here drinking tea' Ally said dreamily. Sally looked at Ally. 'You know what, that isn't such a bad idea' Sally said as she sat a moment and thought about it.

'I was only joking' Ally said, smiling. 'Well, I think it's a great idea' Sally stated as she called John who reappeared at the doorway. 'Change of plan' Sally said. 'What? Already? We haven't even left the cabin! We don't get lost, it is just that you're always changing your mind' John said in jest. 'Get down off your high horse! Ally and I are calling a time out. The kids are going to go with you and Ben whilst we...well, we'll do whatever we want to do' Sally said sternly.

John nodded in acknowledgement. 'OK' he said, before returning back inside. Ally looked across to Molly. 'Is that ok with you?' she said. Molly nodded in agreement. 'You guys had better get your stuff ready before the captain comes back' Sally said, laughing. Hugh, Aden and Molly got up from the table and picked up their plates. 'Don't worry about the washing up, I'll do it in a minute' Ally called after them.

Sally got up too. 'I'd best make sure they are taking the right things' she said as she followed them inside. Ally stood up and moved into the chair next to Ben. Ben leaned back and wrapped his arm around her shoulder. 'You seem more settled today' Ally noticed. Ben smiled. 'I needed this trip just to get my head straight again. There's something about a change of scenery that helps you to get a different view on life' he mused. 'Does it have anything to do with your dad?' Ally cautiously enquired. Ben lifted his arm from around Ally's shoulder and leaned forward.

'There are a few bridges that have been burned in my life. I can forgive but I'm still working on the forgetting part' Ben said, looking at his feet. 'Well, the good thing about bridges is that new ones can always be rebuilt' Ally said, getting up and kissing him on the cheek. She reached for his plate and made her way into the kitchen. Ben sat for a moment looking out at the landscape as the sun shone brightly, listening to the silence. He looked back in Ally's direction. 'I never thought of it like that before' Ben muttered to himself.

Ben took out his phone from his back pocket and began to write a new message: 'I know you only wanted the best for me, that's the reason you pushed me. Even though I resented you when I left, I am grateful for everything you did and taught me even if it's not the way that I would have done it. But I needed to leave to find my own way through this world, to create my own life and see what I could achieve in my own way. I never stopped loving you, pa, it's just that sometimes I didn't always like you. We burned some bridges but maybe we could now start to rebuild some new ones. We'll be back at the ranch this evening and we're having a BBQ with everyone. You could come over and maybe we could make a start on rebuilding those bridges. Ben.' Ben looked at the screen as he read the words back to himself, and pressed send. Ben slipped the phone back in his pocket and walked into the cabin, feeling a weight in his heart begin to lift.

As he walked into the living room he found Aden, Hugh and Molly with their rucksacks and Sally checking through them. 'Aden, you'll need to take your rain jacket just in case' she said. Aden looked out of the window, confused. 'Have you not seen the weather out there? It's sunny!' he protested. 'Weather can change and quickly. Oh, and don't forget to brush your teeth' Sally said, pointing towards his room.

Aden dragged his feet as he made his way towards his room and grabbed his raincoat. He took it with him into the bathroom and walked to the sink where he got his toothbrush and toothpaste. He began to brush his teeth and looked at his reflection in the mirror. He ran his spare hand through his hair and spat out the toothpaste. He rinsed his mouth with water, then wet his hand and ran it through his hair again, causing it to become spiky. Aden stood up taller, pushed his shoulders back and looped his thumbs in his front pockets like he had seen his dad do. As he continued to look at himself he started to see someone different.

He stared at the confident part of himself, as he lifted up his hand and pretended to shake someone's hand. 'Hi, I'm Aden' he said firmly, and looped his thumb back in his jeans. He looked longingly at his reflection and saw for the first time the person he could be. He then reached and grabbed a towel and rubbed his hair dry. His shoulders slumped forward again, returning back to the Aden he knew only too well. He reached and grabbed his coat feeling disheartened, and made his way back into the living room.

Sally turned to Molly as she looked through her bag. 'Yes, you have got everything. Would you mind going to fetch the bottles of water that are cooling in the fridge?' Sally asked. 'Sure' Molly said as she walked to the kitchen. 'OK, Hugh, let's take a look' Sally lifted his bag. 'Wow, what have you got in here? Rocks?' Sally said, struggling to lift it as she looked inside. She saw that the bag was full to the brim. 'No, just the bare essentials' Hugh replied. 'I think you forgot to pack the kitchen sink' Sally said, smiling back at him. 'I would suggest you lighten it a bit because you'll sure get tired quickly carrying that around for a couple of hours' Sally said.

Hugh stood up from the couch and looked in his bag. He rummaged through it and took out a few items before zipping it back up. 'I'll be fine' Hugh said, throwing his bag onto his back. Molly returned to the living room, followed by John and Ben. Molly passed each of them a bottle of water and Aden shoved his jacket in his rucksack. 'Right. Are we good to go?' John said, making his way towards the front door.

Sally kissed Aden on the top of his head. 'Look after him for me' she said, looking across to John. 'Will do' Aden said, giving her a hug before making his way over to the front door. Ally appeared out of the kitchen as she walked over to Hugh and Molly. 'You look out for each other' Ally said with concern. 'Always do, mom' Hugh said, walking across and hugging her before following John and Aden who had made their way outside. Molly began to follow. 'See you in a couple of hours' she said. Ally reached over and hugged her. 'Just no swimming today, alright? I'm nearly out of tea' Ally chuckled. 'I promise' Molly replied considerately, before heading outside.

'I'll go and make us a fresh drink' Sally said, excusing herself from the living room. Ben stepped towards Ally. 'Thank you for earlier. I needed to hear that; I had never thought of it that way before. I kind of got used to the idea that that was how it was meant to be with my pa, but I have invited him over for the BBQ tonight so we can start to rebuild those bridges' Ben said. 'Wow, do you actually mean that for once I helped you?' Ally said, pretending to be shocked.

'Well, I wouldn't go that far' Ben said jokingly. 'I love you, Ally. Even though I probably don't say it often enough, I think it all the time' he said. Ben walked out and closed the front door behind him. 'Ooh ee' Sally said. Ally turned around and saw Sally holding two cups. 'Shall we?' she said, motioning towards the decking. 'Absolutely' Ally said with a spring in her step, as they headed back out onto the decking in the sunshine.

John led the way, followed closely by Aden, Hugh and Molly, with Ben walking at the back. They crossed the road and followed the footpath as it began to climb up the land. Hugh began repeating to himself: 'Every day I am getting better, as I always succeed at what I set out to achieve. I am a champion.' He spoke it to the rhythm of his footsteps as he followed on behind John.

Aden turned round and raised his eyebrows at Molly as they listened to Hugh repeating his new thought over and over again. Molly smiled back, recalling the feeling she had got earlier and the strength it gave her from deep inside. As Molly walked she thought: 'I'm sure that finding the feeling is the way it's meant to be done.'

Ben came up alongside Molly as the climb got steeper and Molly slowed down. 'Come on, we are burning daylight!' John ordered as he powered on, closely followed by Hugh and Aden. Ben looked across at Molly. 'We'll go at our own pace. At least then the world won't look like a blur as it passes us by. We'll get the chance to see the detail' he smiled, as he too slowed down.

'That sounds like a good plan to me' Molly said, stopping to catch her breath. As she looked down at the ground she saw a funny pattern in the soil. Ben followed her gaze then looked up and scanned the land. 'Look over there!' he exclaimed. As Molly followed where Ben was pointing they watched a snake gracefully glide along silently.

Molly froze as she watched the snake disappear. 'You know you can breathe at any point' Ben said jokingly as he saw Molly's mouth clamped shut. Molly took a gasp of air as she looked at Ben, eyes wide with fear. 'There is nothing to worry about, it's harmless' Ben said, as he gently guided her to continue walking.

'Some people say the snake reminds us that there are great healing opportunities around, change, important transitions to be made and with increased energy to create. If you look at it like that then the snake is your friend, your guide' Ben said, as he passed Molly and walked ahead.

Molly stopped for a moment and looked behind her at where the snake had disappeared. 'I don't want to change or make important transitions. I want everything to go back to the way it was' she said to the snake with certainty. 'What's right isn't necessarily what's easiest' Ben called back, before disappearing over the brow of a hill.

Molly quickly scurried after him, not wanting to be left alone where snakes were roaming. As she made it over the brow of the hill she saw everyone sitting down on a cluster of rocks. She walked across, sat down next to Aden, took out her bottle of water and had a drink.

Aden sat distantly looking out onto the horizon as Ben moved across and sat down next to John as they surveyed the map. 'Everything alright?' Molly asked Aden. 'Yes and no' Aden said, feeling disheartened as he rolled his bottle of water between his hands. 'I tried to see myself confidently this morning whilst I was brushing my teeth, and I felt like a fool, like I was just being a kid again, being stupid' Aden said, feeling ashamed.

Molly looked confused. 'Just because it's uncomfortable doesn't mean that it's a bad thing. If everyone stayed the way other people had told and taught them to be then we would all still be living in caves. Believe in what others can't see yet because some day they will see what you have known all along' Molly added, as she placed her bottle back in her rucksack and stood up.

'It's something Nana O taught me' Molly finished, as she watched John and Ben get up too and start to walk again. Molly began to follow as Aden stood up silently, following behind and thinking about Molly's words. Hugh sat still as he watched everyone begin to disappear down the path, continuing to repeat to himself: 'Every day I'm getting better, as I always succeed at what I set out to achieve. I am a champion.' Tears began to roll down his cheeks as the words cut into his heart like a razor blade.

Hugh thought back to all the times that he had failed, when he had missed a shot, or his loop went wrong. All the people watching him that he felt he had let down. 'Every day...' Hugh stuttered. He quickly stood up, violently throwing his bottle of water out in front of him. 'I hate you!' he screamed with pure rage. 'Why can't it be me?' he continued as his face reddened.

As he felt every muscle in his body tighten, his fists clenched as he kicked a lump of dirt and collapsed to his knees. He closed his eyes. 'Why not me, why not now?' he whispered, as a gentle breeze whirled around his face, cooling his tears and stilling his heart.

He heard and felt nothing, as the numbness grew from inside his heart to all around his body. As he scanned around the landscape for guidance and hope, he saw nothing. He continued waiting. 'Hugh, where are you?' he heard John's voice call from a distance. Hugh looked up to the sky. 'You abandoned me. I ask you for help and you leave me here lost when I needed you the most' Hugh said with malice.

He stood up and began to walk down the path, still numb as the darkness grew inside and turned his blood to venom. 'Oh sorry, son' a man apologised as he bumped into Hugh. Hugh stared blankly at him and the man held his gaze. Hugh saw a sparkle in his eyes like he was looking through a keyhole to his heart. 'You know sometimes, son, the only thing we need to do is surrender to this moment, let the hand that created us do its job. Worry is a terrible disease. It distorts and drives us crazy, causing you to no longer hear your guidance, see the opportunities or have the strength to take action. All power and clarity is lost to something that most of the time won't come true' the man said, before walking on by and continuing on his way.

Hugh stood motionless as he awoke from his fury back to reality. He felt the life return in his fingers and legs. 'I surrender. I sort out what we are doing, you sort out how we are going to get there' Hugh said, looking up at the sky before running to catch up with the others.

As the sun reached the top of the sky and the temperature rose, Ben and John scanned the land to see the cluster of log cabins at the bottom of the hill. 'Right you lot, we'd better head back before the ladies think we have got lost' John said, quickening his pace as Molly, Hugh and Aden jogged behind to keep up with him. Ben slowed down as he enjoyed the harmony that surrounded him. He remembered the day he saw the deer whilst out riding, knowing what was awaiting him at the country fair and rodeo.

'I just need a sign' he whispered as he placed his hand in his pocket, holding the small box between his fingers. A noise of small rocks dislodging behind him caused Ben to turn around to see a deer in the centre of the path looking straight at him. Ben stood motionless. 'What have you got to tell me?' he thought as the deer turned round and made its way back up the path.

Ben quickly scurried to follow the deer. As he reached the top of the hill he looked down the other side to see the deer joining another deer with two fawns eating. The deer stopped eating and looked at Ben. Ben crouched down and sat down on the dirt path, watching the four of them peacefully together, a family. A noise came from behind Ben as the deers' heads shot up and they quickly disappeared. Ben turned around and saw Molly standing there.

'Sorry' she said, pointing to the deer running off into the distance. 'We just wondered where you were' Molly said, looking concerned. Ben stood back up. 'I just had to follow something to find an answer' Ben winked at Molly, as he walked past her and followed the path back to the others.

Molly looked at the deer and then back at Ben. 'OK then' she said, feeling confused as she followed Ben. 'Ah, there you are!' John said, raising his hands up in the air. 'Shall we?' he said impatiently as he continued to make his way down the path to the cabins. Ben pretended to salute to John in jest, causing Hugh and Aden to giggle.

Molly reached forward, took hold of Ben's hand and held it tight. 'I thought I had lost you, too' she said quietly. Ben squeezed her hand. 'Not a chance. You'll have to try harder to achieve that' he said, smiling at her. Molly hugged his arm as they neared the cabins.

'Sally, the wonders have returned' Ally called, as she saw them approaching. 'Is that kettle on?' John called back. Ally disappeared as she returned to the kitchen. John stepped onto the decking and plonked himself down in one of the chairs, followed quickly by Hugh and Aden. Molly held tightly onto Ben's arm as they joined everyone on the decking. Sally and Ally returned with plates full of food and drinks, and placed them on the table.

'I'll just go and get that cup of tea for you' Ally said, smiling at John. Ally returned back into the kitchen. Ben peeled Molly's hand off his arm. 'I'll be back in a minute, I just need to speak to Ally' he said as he walked towards the door. He paused and looked back at the table. 'Everyone stay where you are until I say otherwise' Ben said desperately, before heading inside.

As he made his way into the kitchen, Ally was picking up the cup of tea. Ben stepped in towards her and reached for the cup, taking it from her hands and placing it down on the worktop. He looked straight into Ally's eyes with devotion.

Ally became uneasy. 'I have been trying to find the right moment' Ben said, shaking his head at the turmoil he had been fighting inside. 'But I have come to realise that sometimes the perfect moment is disguised in an ordinary moment, that the perfect moment is created by our words and actions. Ally, when I first saw you dancing with Hugh, I turned to Tom and said "That is the women I'm going to marry". I wanted to ask you the first night we met' Ben paused.

Slipping his hand in his jeans pocket, he took out the small box and opened it up. 'Ally, will you do me the absolute honour of becoming my wife? I promise to love you unconditionally, support your dreams, but most of all, every day in every way we will bring out the best in each other' he finished.

Ally stood there staring at the ring sparkling in the

sunshine streaming through the window. She looked at Ben and then back at the ring, then up at Ben again, speechless. Ben took hold of her left hand and gently slid the ring on her finger. Ally nodded, beaming, as she flung her arms around his neck and leaped up into his arms. She stared deep into his eyes as she leaned forward to kiss him.

'Our first forever kiss' Ally said, glowing as Ben whirled her around the kitchen in delight. Ally's smile began to disappear as she climbed out of his arms and took a step back. Ben froze with fear. 'You've not changed your mind already?' he said as he watched her slip off the ring. Ally stared down at the ring she held between her fingers.

As she looked up. 'No, of course not. It's just, I don't think it would be quite right for us to go back to the ranch saying we are going to get married when Molly's parents are splitting up. It's kind of like rubbing salt into the wound' she whispered. Ben sunk his hands deep into his pocket, not able to hide his disappointment. Tears formed in his eyes as he saw Ally holding the ring.

'You're right' Ben said. 'But how about you wear your ring just until we return back to the ranch' he said, searching for hope. 'Ben, I'm forever yours, and just know that it is our words that are the bond binding our hearts. It's the small commitments we honour and keep every day that are just as important as saying

I do' Ally said, slipping the ring back on as she stepped forward and wrapped her arms back around Ben's neck. They swayed in the kitchen to the rhythm of their heartbeats.

'So, this is the secret you have been keeping from me?' Ally said, raising her eyebrows. Ben grinned. 'Well, I wasn't sure how much longer I was going to survive if I kept it from you' he said boldly.

Ally blushed at her earlier behaviour. She reached behind her and took a sip of John's tea. 'Perfect for every situation' he said, taking her hand. 'Absolutely' Ally said, as she intertwined her fingers with his. They stepped out into the living room where they were met by an eruption of cheers. They saw everyone crammed up against the doorway as they had been listening in.

'Finally!' Sally said, breaking free with joy and hugging Ally as John quickly took the cup of tea from Ally before it was tipped onto the floor. John stepped forward and shook Ben's hand. 'Congratulations' he said. Ben beamed with pride. 'Thanks, mate' he replied. Hugh stepped forward and wrapped his arms around both of them. 'I thought I was going to burst if I had to keep the secret much longer' Hugh said, ecstatic. Aden stepped forward and hugged them too.

Molly stayed in the doorway and watched everyone as they celebrated and shined with joy. She turned around and started to walk back to the table. Ben nudged Ally who was twirling around with Hugh. Ben glanced across to where Molly was and Ally nodded as she walked outside and kneeled down in front of Molly.

'Now, every woman needs a bridesmaid and I can't think of anyone better who I would want to be by my side than you. Molly, would you do me the honour of helping me make it through the day?' Ally asked. Molly pretended to brush some dust off her legs as Ben joined Ally, crouching down and wrapping his arm around her waist. 'We want all our family to be part of this and, Molly, you are part of our family' Ben emphasised. Molly began to cry as she nodded and flung her arms around them both. Hugh quickly came up behind, joining in as he wrapped his arms around all three of them.

'At some point I need to take a breath' Ally said, muffled beneath a pile of arms. Everyone began to peel themselves off as Ally gasped for air. As they all returned to their seats, Ben pulled his chair up close to Ally's. He took hold of her hand as he played with the ring with his fingers.

Sally reached under the table and pulled out a bottle of champagne. 'Just a little something to celebrate!' she exclaimed, as she placed it down on the table. She reached across for four glasses she had hidden too. As the cork popped, Sally sprayed Hugh and Aden with the champagne. 'Ah, mom, stop it!' Aden stood up, brushing off the champagne bubbles. Sally poured the champagne into the glasses as John passed one to Ally and then Ben, also taking one for himself. 'Here's to the next chapter, may it be the best one yet' John said, raising his glass up to the sky. This was quickly followed by everyone else raising their glasses of champagne and orange juice.

They sat there in silence, soaking up the sunshine. Then Ally let out a groan as she let her head flop back. Hugh began to laugh as he knew exactly what she was thinking. 'So, when are you going to tell her?' Hugh said, his laugh growing louder. Ally let out a loader groan as Ben began to smirk. 'Not today that's for sure' she said, lifting her head back up to look across at Hugh. 'It's not funny, Monkey. I think you should tell her' Ally said teasingly. 'No way!' he yelled back.

Ally began to laugh too. 'Well, if it is alright with everyone I think we should head back to the ranch and settle in for the BBQ. We'll skip the fishing this time round' Ben said, looking at Ally. 'Sounds good to us' John said, as his body began to ache from the walk earlier on.

'OK, you three can you go and pack up your stuff and put it in the living room' Sally instructed, looking directly at Hugh, Aden and Molly. Hugh opened his mouth to respond and felt a nudge from Ally's foot from under the table. 'Of course, Sally' Hugh said politely. The three of them got up and walked inside to their bedrooms. 'Have you guys had any luck?' Molly asked, agitated.

Hugh and Aden stopped, looking back at Molly. Aden looked down at his feet and shook his head. 'Nope, every time I get close to seeing myself as confident I am then flooded with memories of all the times I wasn't' he said. 'I'm the same. Each time I repeat it I just become angry that I am nowhere near it' Hugh said, disappointed. 'Me too, I can't seem to find the feeling since this morning' Molly said, agreeing. 'What are we doing wrong?' Molly asked. Aden shrugged. 'It beats me!' he exclaimed. They looked at each other in silence.

'I don't hear much movement back there!' Sally called. Aden rolled his eyes. 'I'm sure they are in a constant contest to see who can be the bossiest' he said, quietly looking towards his parents. They all went into their rooms and began to pack up their things.

Ally made her way through and glanced into the bedrooms. She saw the three of them busily shoving their clothes and belongings into their bags. She walked into her own room and sat down on the edge of the bed. She stared at the ring which shimmered and sparkled in the light, like a star in the night sky. Ally felt her heart about to burst with joy and love but at the same time her veins filled with fear. 'What if I lose him too? I wouldn't be able to go on' she mumbled to herself.

'Stop it, Ally, just have a little faith' Ally demanded of herself, as the fear retreated and left her feeling like a child on Christmas day. Ben walked into the room and made his way across to Ally. 'Hello, Mrs' he said, proud of the way that sounded. Ally began to laugh as the joy bubbled out of her. Ben placed his bags on the bed and started to pack his things. 'This is one crazy ride' Ally said, getting up and collecting her belongings. Ben glanced up. 'The best ride there is' he replied.

Molly, Aden and Hugh made their way into the living room, placed their bags down in the centre and flopped on the couch as Sally buzzed in and out with things from the kitchen. 'She makes me feel travel sick sometimes at the rate she moves' Aden said, as Sally whirled in and out like a tornado.

Ben, John and Ally soon joined the three of them and Ben and John started to carry the bags outside to the trucks. 'Do you want some help, dad?' Aden said, watching him walking towards the front door. 'Yep, you can all bring down some bags' John called over his shoulder.

Ally walked into the kitchen and nearly crashed into Sally. 'It's all done' Sally said, herding Ally back out into the living room. Sally brushed passed her and out of the front door. 'Well, I'll go and double check no one has left anything in their rooms' Ally said to herself.

Ally looked around the rooms, closing each door behind her. As she walked back into the living room, having one more glance around, her gaze stopped at the kitchen. 'Tea and a proposal, what more could a woman want?' Ally thought as she made her way out of the front door and closed it behind her. She walked towards the trucks where everyone was waiting.

Ben looked across. 'Good to go?' he asked. 'Good to go' Ally responded. 'OK, kids, time to load up' John bellowed. 'We'll follow you back' John suggested, as Ben climbed into the driver's seat. 'Sure thing' Ben said, starting up the truck as the chime of seatbelts clicked. The truck reversed and turned around as they made their way back down the road towards the exit, with John, Sally and Aden following behind.

Ben reached across and took Ally's hand as the sun shone in a sapphire blue sky and they heard an eagle call from up above. 'Well, life can change pretty quickly around here' Ally said, as she began to watch the countryside roll by. 'I go into Yellowstone as one woman and come back out a completely different one' she smiled across to Ben. 'Well, these places are magical, that's for sure' he replied, as they drove out of the exit gate.

Hugh and Molly looked at each other. 'I wish it had the same effect on me' Hugh said, saddened. Molly smiled in agreement but said nothing.

7 THERE'S NO PLACE LIKE HOME

As the truck cruised down the highway, the four of them sat with just the radio serenading the countryside. Hugh glanced behind him and saw John's truck following on behind. He lifted up his hand and waved; John and Sally waved back in acknowledgement.

Molly began to tap her fingers on the door handle. As her boredom grew, she leaned forward. 'Are we nearly there yet?' she asked, beginning to get fidgety. Ally turned round in her seat, her nose nearly touching Molly's nose. 'Nope, we have hours and hours and hours to go, and then when we have driven that, we still have another hour to go' Ally said teasing her and reaching round and tickling her.

Molly began to laugh. 'Stop stop!' she laughed. Ally turned back round and looked out of the windscreen.

Ben slowed down as they began to drive back through the little town. Ben let out a sigh. 'What is it about this place that gets to you?' Ally asked, looking at Ben's face as it turned to misery.

Ben ran his hand over his face and readjusted his hat. 'Everything' he said distantly, as his gaze looked to each side of the road. 'It's just not a place I'm ready to return to just yet' Ben said as he pressed on the accelerator. The car began to speed up as he reached the stop light, he indicated, turned left and then sped up again, leaving John's truck in the distance. Ally sat silently staring at the enigma Ben was becoming.

Hugh glanced back again to check if John had managed to catch up. He saw John's truck speed up and regroup. Hugh turned back to face the front and caught Ally's attention, looking at her to see what that was all about. Ally just shrugged, not knowing how to respond.

Ben began to slow down and let out a long breath of relief as he turned down the dirt road leading to the ranch. As they watched the countryside blend into a view that had become home, Ally began to smile. It was still as breathtaking as the first time she had seen it.

Molly stiffened in her seat and became rigid. 'STOP!' she yelled at the top of her voice. Ben slammed on the brakes as the truck came to an abrupt halt. Molly's breath started to become rapid as she shook her head from side to side. Ally turned round in her seat and placed her hand on Molly's hand. 'What's wrong sweetheart?' Ally asked Molly, who was now gasping for air. 'I can't do it; I don't want to do it!' she exclaimed. Ally looked across to Ben to see if he knew what she was talking about but he looked just as puzzled. Ally squeezed her hand. 'Don't want to do what, Molly?' she asked soothingly.

Ben looked up and saw Molly's parents out in front of the house. He unclipped his seatbelt and climbed out. He walked round to the back of the truck to Molly's side, opened the door and unclipped her seatbelt. He scooped her up in his arms and rocked her from side to side. 'Molly, I want you to follow my breath' he said. Molly felt Ben's chest slowly rise and fall. She tried to copy but suddenly felt more out of breath and began to breathe rapidly again.

'Just find the rhythm, Molly. You'll have to relax though, you're safe, I've got you' he whispered. Molly closed her eyes and focused on Ben's breath as she started to relax. Tears began to roll down her cheeks. 'I don't want to go back' Molly murmured. 'There is nothing to return to but broken dreams and failures' she finished.

Ben continued to gently rock her from side to side. 'A home isn't a house or the belongings in it, or even the people who live there. Home is where the heart is, where love fills every inch of the space. Where is your heart, Molly?' Ben asked gently. Molly lifted her head up off Ben's shoulder, her eyes red from crying. She looked across the land and then up at the sky. 'Up there' Molly said, feeling peace wash over her.

'From now on, when you want feel home just look up at the stars' Ben said, smiling. Molly nodded and sat back in her seat. Hugh moved across and hugged her. 'I know you can do this, Molly, you're really brave.' Ben stepped back, closed the door and waved to John that everything was OK. Ben climbed back into the truck and continued down the dirt road before pulling up in front of the house next to a familiar truck. He paused as he himself became anxious.

Ben turned off the ignition and turned round in his seat to look back at Molly. 'How about we both be really brave over the next few hours and try to be someone new together?' he said. Molly smiled wearily in agreement as she took a deep breath and opened the door. 'Hey you, did you have a good trip?' Molly's mum came over, wrapping her arms around Molly.

'Yes, thank you' Molly said quietly, as her mum stepped back and her dad came over and hugged her. 'Well, I'll get the kettle on' Molly's mum announced as she began to make her way back into the house. Ally and Hugh stepped out of the truck. 'Great idea' Ally agreed. John's truck pulled up and Sally, John and Aden stepped out and walked across to Molly's dad. 'Hi, pleased to meet you. I'm John, this is Sally and Aden' John introduced. 'Hi' Molly's dad replied, shaking his hand.

'Come on everyone, it's BBQ time' Hugh said, grabbing Sally and John's hands and pulling them into the house. They were quickly followed by Ally, Aden and Molly's dad. Molly stared back at Ben who was still sitting in the truck, staring across to the barn as he watched two men walking towards the house. Ben looked back towards the house and smiled at Molly encouragingly. Molly stared for a moment before turning and heading into the house.

Ben opened the door and stepped out. As he closed the door he was greeted by Tom. 'How was your trip? At least you survived it' he said, holding out his hand and shaking it with Ben's. 'Life changing' Ben replied, smiling. 'Good on you mate, finally' Tom said beaming. 'Did she say yes?' Tom asked jokingly. Ben playfully tapped him on the shoulder in response. 'Was everything alright here?' he asked, glancing across the ranch. 'Of course it was, I was looking after it' Tom said as he brushed past and walked into the house.

As Tom walked away, Ben walked towards Billy. Ben shuffled uncomfortably. 'I'm not sure how we are meant to start rebuilding these bridges, son' Billy said, sinking his hands deep into his jeans pockets. 'You being here tonight is a great start' Ben replied hopefully. 'Congratulations, on the...' Billy said, pointing towards the front door. 'You sure have created a nice spot for yourself here' he said as he looked at the house.

Ben turned and looked in the same direction. 'It's become a home I always dreamed of and wanted' he replied, before turning and grabbing the bags from the back of the truck. 'Here, let me help you with that' Billy stepped forward and took a bag from his hands. Ben smiled as they walked into the house and put the bags down in the living room.

'I'd better introduce you' Ben suggested, as they walked together into the kitchen. As they entered the room everyone fell silent. Ben stepped forward and coughed gently, clearing his throat. 'Everyone, I would like you to meet my pa, Billy.' Billy gingerly lifted up his hand in a suggested wave to everyone.

Hugh jumped off the chair and went across to hug Billy. 'Hi, it's good to see you again so soon' and Molly quickly followed, hugging him too. Hugh motioned across to Aden to come over. 'This is our friend Aden, he is on the journey too' Hugh said, winking at Billy.

'The trio, now why does this look familiar?' Billy said, looking across to Ben. Ben smirked. 'I am going to light the BBQ' he said, making himself scarce. 'Hi' Molly's mum got up, walked across to Billy and shook his hand. 'We're Molly's parents' she said pointing to Molly's dad. 'It's a pleasure to meet you, mam' Billy replied.

Ally continued to stare at Billy, still undecided on how she felt about him. Billy stared back and walked across towards her. Ally stiffened. 'I think we got off on the wrong foot' Billy said as he stood next to her chair. Ally stared down then slid her chair back and stood up. Billy glanced down at her finger, noticing his grandmother's ring.

He took Ally's hand as he looked at the ring and smiled sweetly. He opened his arms wide, pulling her in close and hugging her tight. 'Welcome home and to the family' he whispered. Ally began to relax as she looked up and smiled. 'Thank you, I'm looking forward to this new chapter in my life' she said.

Then her face turned to shock as she suddenly realised that she was still wearing the ring and plunged her left hand into her pocket. 'Oh, don't you try and hide it, Missy' Molly's mum began. 'You could spot that rock from a mile off, I was just waiting for you tell me' Molly's mum said, placing her hands on her hips.

Ally stepped away and across to Molly's mum. 'I just... I didn't want to cause any problems' she said sheepishly. 'Don't be so daft, we are getting a divorce and we are both in agreement that this is the best course for our paths, but most of all, why can't a relationship end on a good note?' Molly's mum protested. Ally hugged Molly's mum. 'It can and it should' Ally said.

They heard Ben's footsteps walking across the living room as he re-entered the kitchen. Molly's dad stood up. 'Congratulations, great news' he said, stepping across and patting Ben on the back. Ben stood looking confused and then looked across to Ally. Ally lifted up her left hand and wiggled her fingers. 'Oh, right, yes' Ben stuttered.

'It's about time mate, you were driving us all crazy never shutting up about it' Tom said. 'Good job I got this yesterday, just in case' he said as he walked across to the fridge, opened it and took out a bottle of champagne.

'Well, I think we should take this outside' Ben suggested, as he walked across to the kitchen cupboard and took out six glasses. Ally picked up three of them as Ben, Molly's parents and Tom walked across the living room and out onto the back porch. Billy stood in the kitchen looking at the trio. 'How has it been going?' he asked inquisitively.

Hugh looked across to Molly and then Aden. 'Terrible' Molly replied. 'We get a glimpse of it and then it disappears, and we can't get it back.' Billy stood quietly listening. 'We decided that Aden was to practise seeing it, Hugh to think it, and me to feel it' Molly continued. 'And it still didn't work' Hugh said in frustration.

Billy grunted then turned and walked out of the front door. He made his way to the back of his truck. Hugh, Aden and Molly walked across the kitchen and watched out of the kitchen window. Billy lifted something out from the back of his truck covered in a sheet, and walked back towards the front door.

Hugh, Aden and Molly darted back to their original spot, looking innocent. As Billy entered he motioned for them to come into the living room, as he placed the object down on the couch and lifted off the sheet.

Molly, Hugh and Aden stared at the mirror. 'I don't get it' Aden said, looking back at Billy. Molly stepped forward and put her finger against the mirror. 'It's the mirror of miracles' she said. Ben walked back into the living room and stopped suddenly in his tracks as he spotted the mirror, causing him to freeze.

'This mirror has helped our family to achieve success, love and happiness for generations' Billy said, crouching down. 'This is the mirror that Ben's grandpa stood him in front of and told him the same truth that I told you: the person you see is the person you'll be' Billy said carefully.

Ben walked across the room. As he reached the

mirror he ran his fingers around the edge as the memories of him as a little boy standing in front of the it flooded back. All the wishes made, tears shed and words spoken, as now he stood looking at the picture being reflected back to him with Hugh, Molly and Aden by his side. 'Some journey' he muttered, as he turned and looked back at Billy.

Billy's eyes glistened as they began to fill with tears of pride. Ben turned back to look at Hugh, Molly and Aden. 'My grandpa said to me when he first took me to this mirror: "to truly believe is to have faith in something others can't see as we are all on a journey remembering who we are meant to be"' he said serenely. Billy stepped forward. 'Sometimes when you are dreaming you reach the place where you no longer need it to be part of your reality because the joy you feel just thinking about it is enough. All you were searching for was to feel happy' Billy placed his hand on Ben's shoulder and smiled.

'But I don't get why it isn't working' Hugh said, stepping in front of Ben. 'What are you doing?' Ben asked, crouching down. 'I'm using words and keep repeating them to myself: that I am a champion. Molly is feeling home and Aden is seeing himself as confident. We're hoping that these things can come true, that thoughts become things' Hugh said.

Ben beamed with a smile. 'If I was to throw a baseball at this mirror, what would happen?' Ben asked. 'It would crack and some pieces may even fall off' Aden answered. 'I agree, let's say that the baseball is a difficult time in our lives' Ben continued. 'Then you need to rebuild the mirror, putting the pieces back together, one by one. Our tears that fall stick the broken pieces of ourselves back together that lay all around us on the floor. Then our love, hope and belief in ourselves, that greater part of ourselves, fill in and mend the cracks, until one day the picture is once again complete and whole' Ben said, as he looked at each of them.

Aden walked across and stood looking at the mirror. 'The triangle' he responded. Ben nodded as he watched Aden begin to find the answers. 'What is a thought?' Aden asked, looking at Ben and Billy. 'Now you're asking the right question' Billy replied. 'A thought is a word, a feeling, and a picture' he continued.

Molly suddenly looked up at Billy. 'We are meant to do all three together, not separately' she said. Ben stood up and stepped back, standing next to Billy. 'Keep going' he encouraged. 'If I speak about my home, feel the feeling of home and see myself walking through the front door of my home, that's when it starts to come true' she continued, as she looked back at herself in the mirror. 'Correct! Most people try one but forget the other two, but when all three are lined up and used then miracles begin to happen' Ben said.

Molly stayed quiet and continued to look at herself in the mirror as she truly thought about home. She felt a whirl of something spin around her. Ben looked across at Billy. 'She's got it' Billy nodded in agreement. 'I think it's time for this to come to you' Billy said, looking at Ben and then at the mirror. 'So you too can pass it down from father to son' he continued, pointing to Hugh. Ben hugged Billy tightly. 'Thank you, pa' he said with delight.

Hugh stepped up next as he too thought about being a world champion, as he felt life pulsate around him and his fears and worries vanish. He turned round to look at Ben, beaming. 'I get it, I get it!' he bounced around, hugging Molly. Aden timidly stepped forward and looked at his reflection but felt discomfort. 'I'll be back in a minute' he said as he disappeared into the bathroom. He turned on the tap and started wetting his hair.

He quickly returned and stood back in front of the mirror. His smile began to grow as he lifted his chin, relaxed his shoulders and let out a sigh as he nodded to himself in approval. Hugh and Molly wrapped their arms around him in delight as they all realised the truth.

'May I?' Ben asked, stepping forward and looking at himself in the mirror. 'Mirror, mirror, on the wall. No longer shall you reflect the person I once was, as now I stand tall, seeing for the first time a truth like never before. As the veil is lifted between the worlds and I see there in the reflection the person I was and am in the dream world' Billy started to speak the words with Ben. 'As the light inside my heart begins to shine, illuminating every part of my life as now I find the person in my dreams, is standing there staring back at me' Ben stared intensely at his reflection. There before his eyes he saw himself transform into the man he dreamed to be each day.

'You're going to have to teach me that' Molly said in awe. 'You need to set the space for transformation to take place' Ben said, making his way into the kitchen. Billy followed Ben as he entered the kitchen and leaned on his elbows on the back of the kitchen chair.

'Well, that scene sure did look familiar' Billy remarked. Ben lifted the meat out of the fridge and placed it on the worktop. 'Who would have known that it would all come back round, full circle' Ben said, looking with disbelief. Billy smiled as they said in unison: 'grandpa', as they both started to laugh.

Billy moved across, picked up some of the meat and was followed by Ben as they walked across the living room. 'Come on you three, you can come back to that later' Ben instructed. They all made their way out of the patio doors to where John was busy at the BBQ. Ben and Billy put the meat down and sat down at the table.

'So, Billy, can you tell us a story about Ben, because he never tells us anything about himself?' Hugh said, resting his arms on the table. 'Come on, Monkey, just let Billy settle in first before you start your interrogation' Ally instructed. 'Actually, I agree with Hugh' Molly seconded. Molly's mum looked across disapprovingly.

Billy leaned back in his chair and laid his foot on his knee. 'Oh, don't worry, I don't mind' Billy said, getting comfy. Ben began to look worried. 'Well, there was this one time, when Ben was little and he was riding this little black pony and that pony had the measure of him. I had tried to tell Ben to get control of those feet before those feet walked him straight into trouble. But he was having none of it' Billy said, chuckling at Ben.

Ben bowed his head as he remembered the day well. Billy continued. 'Well, the next thing I knew I saw this little black pony bucking across the field and Ben looking like a pea on a drum. It didn't take too long before Ben had his first taste of flying and as he landed, his head fell straight into a fresh pile of poo' Billy began roaring with laughter, instantly followed by Tom who laughed too, neither of them able to talk.

'And broke my leg in the process' Ben continued. 'Tried and tested horse poo isn't for eating' he said. The whole table erupted into a chorus of laughter.

Ben began to blush. 'Talk about getting what you deserve. I knew that pony wasn't ready to be ridden that day but I thought I'd try' Ben finished, starting to laugh himself. 'But, heck, from that day on I always have control of the horses' feet before I swing up into the saddle' Ben said, crossing his arms across his chest.

The laughter began to die down as John walked across with a pile of burgers, steaks and sausages and placed them on the table. 'Food's ready' he announced. The plate was passed around. As it reached Ben, Hugh said cheekily 'Do you want some horse poo with that Ben?' and everyone started to laugh again. Ben stayed quiet. 'And there was me thinking it would be a good idea to have you over' Ben said sarcastically to Billy.

'It's through our stories that we learn the most' Billy replied, before taking a bite from his burger. Billy turned to Molly's parents. 'So, how long are you staying for?' Billy asked politely. Molly's dad paused before taking a bite of steak and placing his fork back on the plate. 'Well, actually, we are heading back tomorrow. Something has come up back in England' he said.

Ally looked across to Molly's mum. 'So soon!' she said nervously. 'It's for the best. I know it's only been a flying visit but I'm sure it won't be long before we are back again' she said. 'I'm not going' Molly said sternly. 'Now come on, Molly, we don't need to make a fuss out of this' Molly's dad said, looking intensely at her.

'I'm not dad but I am not going and that's the end of it' Molly said, folding her arms across her chest and glaring at her dad. 'This isn't open for discussion, Molly' Molly's mum stepped in. 'You're right, mum, it's not. I'm not going, I am staying here, even if it's for another week or month, but I am not leaving tomorrow' Molly retorted.

Molly's mum took a deep breath, trying to stay calm. 'Look, young lady, I know you didn't ask for all this but your dad and I need to go back to England tomorrow because we have arranged to see the lawyers the following day' Molly's mum hissed. 'Well, have fun with that, I will catch a different plane and stay here until then' Molly said casually, getting up from the table and walking inside.

Molly's mum glared at Molly's dad. Ally piped up. 'If you want, Molly is more than welcome to stay here for a little while and we'll drop her off at the airport and even walk her to the plane' she said. 'She is too young' Molly's mum erupted. 'That kid knows more about life and is more clued up than we are' Molly's dad replied.

'I am not arguing with you about this, she is coming home with us tomorrow and that's the end of it'

Molly's mum scolded. 'You're right, we aren't going to argue over this. Let's try for once in our lives to be adults. Don't you think that it's probably best if Molly stays out of the way whilst we make these decisions' Molly's dad replied. 'No, I think she should be part of this' Molly's mum said, looking bewildered at the obscurity of his remark.

Molly came back outside with a drink in her hand and sat back down at the table. 'I agree with dad, I do not want to be part of you two unstitching our family and life, I have my own journey and path to take and that starts here' Molly said, pointing to the house.

Molly's mum stared at Molly as her words pierced her heart and she quietly returned to eating. Ben, Sally, John, Hugh, Tom and Aden sat quietly as the storm of emotions whirled around the table. An eerie stillness descended as everyone remained uncomfortably quiet. As Molly's mum lifted a fork full of food to her mouth, she looked over and saw a white feather lying on her plate. She paused, picking it up and glanced up at an empty sky. Molly looked across. 'See, even Nana O thinks I should stay' she said.

Molly's mum was just about to share her thoughts of how bogus the thought was, but remained quiet as she realised that was the only hope Molly had at the moment. Molly's dad took hold of Molly's mum's hand and squeezed it gently. 'I think Molly should get to choose. At least then we know where she is' he said, as he remembered the day Molly ran off from school to Nana O's cottage.

'We'll take good care of her and make sure she gets back to you safe' Ben said, as he looked sympathetically across to them. 'You can get back on a plane at any point' Ally added. 'This is really what you want? To stay here?' Molly's mum asked one final time.

Molly nodded as she looked across the pasture and the mountain in the background. 'Yes, I feel like I have come home' she whispered. Molly's mum began to cry as she got up from the table and quickly made her way inside, followed by Ally. 'Honey, you know you will always have a home with us' Molly's dad replied, trying to hold back his tears.

'I know, dad' she said, getting off her chair, climbing onto his knee and wrapping her arms around his neck. 'But here is the place that I call home' Molly replied with relief as the words she spoke finally aligned with her true thoughts. 'OK then' Molly's dad squeezed her tight.

Tom looked at the empty wine bottle on the table. 'How about I go and get us another one' he said, finding an excuse to step away from the drama. Ben looked up. 'That sounds a good idea' he said encouragingly. Tom walked into the kitchen where he found Ally and Molly's mum deep in discussion, sitting at the kitchen table with a cup of tea. He quietly lifted a bottle off the wine rack, trying to stay unnoticed, and escaped back into the living room.

As he walked past the couch he looked down and saw the mirror. Stopping in his tracks he slowly made his way back round the couch and stared at the mirror. 'You son of a gun, where did you come from?' he said, shocked.

He began to walk back to the table outside, flooded with memories. He stepped out through the patio doors and paused, pointing back at the living room as he stared at Billy and Ben. 'Well, that's a blast from the past' he said, still in disbelief.

Ben turned round. 'It sure is. Do you remember when we used to spend each morning in front of that mirror?' Ben reminisced. 'Sure do, boy that thing turned our life around' Tom said, sitting back down in his chair and placing the bottle of wine on the table. 'What did you use it for?' Aden asked curiously.

Tom looked up at the sky. 'Well, when we were young lads we used to go out competing at the rodeos and we sucked big style. Our names always sat at the bottom of the table. One year we even got a prize for always being last. Back then we were complete failures' Tom said, as he recalled the past. 'And then Billy took us to see grandpa, as we all knew him as, and grandpa took us into his office where all his trophies, buckles and cheques lined the walls. Ben and I sat there crying our hearts out as we had just returned from another epic disaster at the rodeo' Tom said, as he looked down at his hands as the feeling of despair returned.

'That's when grandpa took us to the mirror and told us: "Who you see is who you'll be, start to see a winner, and you'll start to be a winner. Just practise your new story every day like you are auditioning to play the lead role in a movie of your life"' Tom said. 'Well, Ben and I went to that mirror every morning, seeing, speaking and feeling like winners. And, what seemed like forever at the time but was actually within a season, little by little things started to change. We got a win at our next rodeo' Tom said proudly. 'Then we lost the next five' Ben interrupted. 'But we didn't let that distract us from our new story of who we wanted to be' Tom interjected. 'And within a few more rodeos we were starting to get more wins than failures until we reached the championships' Tom continued. 'Wow! So within a season, you won the championships?!' Hugh exclaimed.

'Not quite, that year we came last at the championships. I guess a part of us was still playing out the old story but, like Tom said, it didn't distract us, we continued to stand in front of the mirror truly thinking who we were meant to be winners. Then the following year we had straight wins. Every rodeo we went to we won, including the championships' Ben said, as he reached and started to pour out the wine.

'And you practically lived with us that entire year' Billy added, looking at Tom. 'We earned our keep and grandpa made the most of having two young lads around to help with the ranch' Tom replied. 'That's true' Billy agreed.

Hugh sat back in amazement. 'It is possible, isn't it?' he said. Ben nodded. 'A miracle is when something extraordinary happens anyway, and that's how it got its name: the Miracle Mirror' Ben said. 'I'll drink to that' Tom said, lifting up his glass. They all raised their glasses and said 'Cheers!' as the glasses chimed together.

Molly's mum and Ally returned and sat back down at the table. Molly got up and walked across, hugging her mum. 'It doesn't mean I don't love you' she said. Molly's mum pulled her up onto her lap. 'I know, it's just a lot of change in what feels like a short space of time and I'm just readjusting to it' she said, hugging Molly.

'I'm going to have to excuse myself, it's been a long day' Molly's mum said, lifting Molly back onto her chair as she stood up. 'And we still need to pack' Molly's mum said, looking at Molly's dad. Molly's dad stood up and put down his glass. 'We'll say goodnight, it was a pleasure to meet you, Billy' Molly's dad said, holding out his hand. 'Hope to see you again sometime' Billy replied, standing up and shaking his hand.

'Definitely' Molly's dad replied, before they headed inside and upstairs to pack. 'Well, I'd better be heading off too. I've still got things to finish at the ranch' Billy announced. Ben stood up, moved across and hugged Billy. 'Thanks for coming over, you're welcome anytime' Ben said. 'I love you, son' Billy said, patting Ben on the back. 'Love you too, pa' Ben replied.

Tom stood up. 'I'll head out with you' he said, looking at Billy. 'See you around' Tom said, hugging Ben. 'Oh, and well done' he finished, glancing across at Ally. Ben smiled gleefully as he playfully pushed Tom through the door, followed by Billy. 'What an evening' Sally said, as she picked up the bottle of wine. John quickly took it back out of her hand. 'We had better be setting off as well' he said, looking prudently at Sally. 'Right, well then let me help you clear up' Sally said, as she started to collect the plates. 'Don't worry about that, we'll leave them on the side and sort them out in the morning, I'm beat' Ally said as she yawned.

They all got up from the table and carried the plates and dishes into the kitchen. They saw Tom and Billy pull off in their trucks and head off down the dirt road. As they placed the dishes on the side, Sally turned to Ally. 'We look forward to receiving our invite' she said excitedly, hugging her. 'We'll be seeing you before then, that's for sure' Ally insisted.

'Anytime you want to head over, the door's always open' John said as he hugged Ben. Molly, Aden and Hugh walked into the living room and took one final glance in the mirror. Hugh placed an arm on each of their shoulders. As they stood there looking at their reflection, nothing needed to be said as the picture of their reflection said it all.

'Come on, you' Sally said, poised at the front door. Aden hugged Hugh and Molly. 'See you again soon' he said, before following Sally and John out of the front door. Ally followed behind and as she, Hugh and Molly stood in the doorway they waved and watched John's truck travel up the dirt road.

Ally stepped back into the house. 'Right, you two, time to hit the apple and pears and scoot up those stairs' she said. Molly and Hugh giggled as they ran across the living room and up the stairs to get ready for bed. Ben stood in the kitchen, staring confused at Ally. 'The apple and pears?' he asked, bewildered. Ally started to giggle too. 'It's an English saying' she said, brushing over the remark.

'I'll see you up there' Ally said before following on behind as she headed up the stairs. As she reached the landing she was greeted by Hugh coming out of the bathroom in his pj's. Ally walked into Hugh's bedroom as he climbed into his bed and she pulled up his duvet. She looked up at his vision wall. 'We have come a long way since that first day, Monkey. I am so proud of you' Ally said, kissing him goodnight. Ben appeared at the door and sat down on the bed beside Ally. 'Thanks for all your help today, champ' Ben said warmly.

'Can I show you something?' Hugh said, climbing from under his duvet. As he faced his vision wall he slowly unstuck a poster and there underneath was a collection of pictures of a wedding and in the centre the photo of Ben, Ally and Hugh at the country fair and rodeo where they first met. Ally's mouth fell wide open. Ben began to laugh. 'I should have known you'd have something to do with this!' Ally exclaimed, as she then turned round to Ben. Ben held up his hands in protest, 'I knew nothing I promise!'

Hugh plonked back down on his bed as Ally reached across and began to tickle him. 'Stop, mom, stop!' he bellowed. Ally gave him one final kiss. 'You are sneaky. I'm going to have to keep an eye on you' she said, pointing at him as she got up and walked out of the room. Ben shuffled across. 'You are a true champion, thanks for the help' he said, looking up at the vision wall. 'Love you' Hugh said. 'Love you to the stars and back' Ben said, hugging him tight before getting up and walking back out onto the landing and closing the door behind him. He found Ally giving Molly a kiss goodnight.

Ben walked towards Molly. 'Goodnight, Miracle Molly' he said. 'Night' Molly smiled, as she skipped into her room and closed the door. 'I'll meet you in there' Ally said, motioning towards the bedroom. 'I just want to check they have everything they need' Ally said, as she looked towards where Molly's parents were. Ben smiled as he tucked a piece of Ally's hair behind her ear and made his way into the bedroom.

Ally stepped across and lightly knocked on the door. 'It's only me' Ally whispered. 'Come in' Ally heard Molly's mum reply. Ally walked into the bedroom. 'I just wanted to check you had everything' as she watched Molly's dad close the suitcase, then perch on the bed. 'Yes, thanks. Are you sure you're alright with this?' he asked, concerned.

'Absolutely. It will keep Hugh out of mischief' Ally remarked. 'Well, I'm not sure about that' Molly's mum said doubtfully. 'I'll run you to the airport, what time is your flight?' Ally asked. 'Gates open at 7am' Molly's dad said, glancing at the tickets on the bedside table. 'OK, perfect. We'll get you there in plenty of time, goodnight' Ally said, as she walked back out onto the landing and closed the door behind her, hearing Molly's parents' voices in the background.

As she walked to her bedroom, Ally began to hum her favourite tune. She changed into her pj's and slipped under the duvet. Letting out a large sigh, her body relaxed and she melted into the bed. She felt the bed hugging her back. The en suite door opened as Ben appeared. He walked across, climbed into bed next to her and wrapped his arms around her. He kissed her on the cheek. 'Night night, Mrs' he said. Ally smiled as her eyelids became heavy and she drifted off to sleep.

Ally's eyes shot open as the chime of her alarm rang in her ears. She groggily opened her eyes and looked at the time. 'Oh, three o' clock, I didn't know there was one of those in the morning' she sighed as she peeled back the duvet. She manoeuvred her way through the dark, scooped up her clothes and walked across to the bathroom. She glanced back at Ben who was still fast asleep.

Ally quickly got dressed and tip-toed out of the bathroom. She headed out of the bedroom and onto the landing where Molly's dad was just leaving his bedroom with a suitcase in each hand. 'Morning' he whispered. 'Morning is at 7am' Ally said sarcastically. As they made their way down the stairs, Molly's dad placed the suitcases by the front door and headed into the kitchen.

Molly's mum was placing three fresh cups of tea on the table. 'Oh, you're an angel' Ally said, picking up and nursing the warm cup of tea. 'Is Molly coming with us?' Ally asked as she took a sip of tea. 'No, we thought it would be best for her to stay here. We sorted everything out last night' Molly's mum replied. Ally nodded. 'It's probably for the best. I'm sure Hugh has organised a whole bunch of surprises for them to do today, so she might as well get a good night's sleep' Ally said, as she recalled what Hugh had been hiding on his vision wall.

Molly's dad glanced at the clock on the wall. 'I'll go and put those in the truck' he said, moving towards the front door and picking up the suitcases. Ally glanced round. 'You're right, we'd better be heading off' she said, as she gulped her tea. Ally and Molly's mum walked towards the front door. Molly's mum took Ally's hand and paused for a moment. 'You have been so incredible and I am so glad you finally get to live the life you dreamed of, especially after what happened to Hugh's dad' she said. Ally got teary as she looked around the living room. 'Me too. It wasn't easy but it was definitely the right thing to do' she smiled, as she placed her hand on Molly's mum's shoulder.

'Maybe I could borrow your strength for a while' Molly's mum said in jest. 'Oh, you're a firecracker, you'll make it through this, you'll see' Ally said, as they stepped out into the cool night air with the stars twinkling in the sky. Molly's dad slid into the truck followed by Molly's mum and Ally. Ally started up the truck, turned it round and headed down the dirt road, glancing from time to time at the animals sleekly moving through the darkness.

As they began to see signs for the airport the sky celebrated the arrival of a new day as the sunrise filled the sky with bright reds and oranges. 'Oh, isn't it beautiful' Molly's mum said as she leaned forward, admiring the sky. 'It sure is, no sunrise is ever the same, just like each day' Ally said, also admiring the changing colours in the sky. Ally headed up the slip road that led to the airport. She manoeuvred her way around until she parked under the "Departures" sign and turned off the ignition. They all got out and Molly's dad lifted the suitcases from the back of the truck. 'Well, I guess this is goodbye' Molly's mum said. 'Thanks for everything' she whispered, as she hugged Ally. 'It's not goodbye, just see you later' Ally replied, as she held Molly's mum tight. Molly's mum stepped back, allowing Molly's dad to hug Ally. 'Just give us a call if anything goes wrong with Molly and we'll sort things out for her to fly back' he said, staring straight at Ally. 'Absolutely, but I don't think anything is going to go wrong' Ally said confidently.

Molly's mum gave Ally one final hug before they disappeared through the departure doors. Ally leaned against the truck and watched them vanish into the crowds. Ally got back into the truck and turned on the ignition. Hearing the truck come to life and pressing the accelerator caused the truck to roar in response, which in turn caused her to giggle. 'I never get tired of that' she said to herself, as she pulled off and drove towards the exit sign.

As Ally rolled down the highway, the sky was bright blue and the sun climbed higher in the sky. She turned on the radio and tapped her fingers on the steering wheel to the beat of the song. Ally became lost in thought at the endless possibilities that lay ahead and of things that may be just around the corner. 'Oh no!' Ally thought, as she remembered she still needed to make the phone call to tell her mother the wedding news.

She turned off the highway and drove towards the dirt road. 'Just do it, Ally' she instructed herself. She pressed the car phone and typed in the number. The phone's ring echoed around the truck. 'Don't pick up, don't pick up' Ally muttered to herself. Then she heard: 'Beep… please leave a message after the tone. If you would like to re-record your message at any point then press the hash key.' Ally started speaking: 'Hi, mom, just a quick call to say Hugh's great. Molly and Co came over, Molly is now living with us for a few weeks as Molly's parents are getting a divorce and are just on their way back to England. Oh, and I'm getting married, bye.' Ally quickly ended the phone call and let out a loud sigh of relief.

Ally turned down the dirt road as she looked around her. 'Home' she said sweetly to herself, as she continued along and saw the horses grazing in the pasture with the mountain bold and strong in the background. Ally pulled up in front of the house, turned off the ignition and stepped out of the truck.

She slowly made her way to the front door and let out a yawn as she stepped through into the house. Her nose was filled with the smell of pancakes and her stomach rumbled with delight.

Ally walked into the kitchen to find Ben sitting at the table with his coffee, whilst Hugh and Molly whirled around making pancakes. 'Hey, mom, you're just in time' Hugh said, placing the stack of pancakes in the centre of the table. Ally slid into one of the chairs as her stomach rumbled again more loudly.

Ally reached across, placed a pancake on her plate, poured the maple syrup on top and quickly ate it, as Molly and Hugh came to sit down too. Ally reached for another pancake. 'Hungry, mom, by any chance?' Hugh said, raising his eyebrows. 'Hey, I have already been up for hours' Ally protested, as she took another bite.

'Did they get off alright?' Ben enquired. Ally nodded with her mouth full of food, and then glanced across at Molly who was sitting smiling. Ally looked up at Ben for answers. 'So, what are you two up to today?'

Ben asked, as he drowned his pancake in maple syrup, rolled it up and put it in his mouth. 'Can we take Firefly and Red Rock up to the place you took me?' Hugh asked. Ben placed his fork down as he leaned back, stretching his stomach in satisfaction. 'Sure, you know what I think? That would be a great idea!' Ben replied, as he remembered Hugh's first few days at the ranch and taking him up there.

'Brilliant' Hugh said, shoving the last piece of pancake in his mouth and placing the plate in the dishwasher. Molly quickly followed. 'Here you go, you can borrow these' Hugh said, thrusting a pair of boots at Molly again. 'Just hold on a minute' Ben said, getting up from the table. Hugh looked across inquisitively. 'We might as well keep up the tradition' Ben said, disappearing into his office and returning with two bags.

Hugh slid his boots, coat and cowboy hat on, beaming as he walked over to sit down on Ally's knee as they watched. Molly looked across at him for guidance. Ben placed the bags on the table. 'You see, Miss Molly, Hugh started a bit of a tradition around here' Ben began, as he took out a pair of cowgirl boots and held them in front of Molly. He then took out a belt and buckle with flowers and a horse's head on it and placed it on the table whilst Molly slipped on her boots. Then finally, Ben placed a cowgirl hat on Molly's head whilst she threaded the belt through the loops of her jeans.

Molly stood up tall, glowing with happiness. 'How do I look?' she said as she paraded around the kitchen. 'Like someone who's ready to do some work around here' Ben said, looping his thumbs in his jeans pocket.

Molly froze and groaned. 'Come on, Molly, let's go for a ride' Hugh said, grabbing her hand and pulling her out of the front door. Ally and Ben watched them run across to the barn. 'When did you get those?' Ally asked as she got up to load up the dishwasher. 'Oh, I texted Tom whilst we were at Yellowstone to ask him to pick them up when he passed the store. I had a feeling we would be needing them' Ben said, looking back across towards the barn.

Ally paused and looked across at Ben. 'What do you know that I don't?' Ally asked curiously. Ben glanced across at her. 'It's just a feeling' Ben said distantly, before walking towards his office. Ally watched him disappear into the office and then looked back at the barn. 'What is around that next corner?' she muttered cautiously.

Hugh walked into the tack room, lifted a saddle off the rack and handed it to Molly. 'Here, you can use this one' he said, as Molly scooped her hands underneath the saddle. 'This is heavy' she said, as her arms instantly began to ache. Hugh lifted off another saddle and began to make his way out of the tack room. 'You'll get used to it' he said, as Molly followed behind. She copied Hugh and placed the saddle on a rack outside the stable. Hugh slid the bolt across on Red Rock's stable door and walked inside. 'Come on' Hugh motioned. 'She's really gentle' he said.

Molly tentatively stepped in and stood next to Hugh. She reached up and ran her fingers along Red Rock's fur. 'It's so soft' she said, smiling at Hugh. Hugh walked out of the stable and returned with the saddle. As he lifted it into the stable, Ben appeared at the stable door. 'Let me give you a hand with that' Ben stepped in and swung the saddle up. Hugh went round the other side and let down the cinch, as Ben reached and cinched up.

'Do you want to go and get their bridles whilst I put Firefly's saddle on?' Ben asked, as he left the stable and moved next door. Molly continued to run her fingers along Red Rock's shoulder, feeling the warmth beneath her fingers. Hugh returned holding a bridle. He gently asked Red Rock to lower her head and he slipped on the bridle. He led Red Rock out into the alley. 'Here you go' Hugh said, handing the reins over to the Molly.

'What am I supposed to do with these?' Molly asked. Ben walked out of Firefly's stable and came across to Molly, scooping her up and placing her in the saddle. Hugh headed over to Firefly to bridle her. 'Left, right, stop, back' Ben said as he placed the reins in Molly's hands and moved them around.

'OK, I think I have got it' Molly said, staring intensely as she practised moving her hand from side to side. Hugh brought Firefly out and walked across to the hay bales as he climbed into the saddle. 'Could you open the gate for us?' Hugh asked, as he motioned for Firefly to walk forward. Red Rock began to follow as Molly quickly grabbed onto the saddle horn. Ben walked by her side. 'You alright up there?' he asked, watching her knuckles go white.

Molly continued to stare ahead at Hugh and Firefly. Ben quickened his pace, opened the gate and leaned on it. Hugh and Molly rode by. 'Have a great ride, guys' Ben said, as he closed the gate behind them. As they began to climb up the hill, Hugh glanced behind him to see Molly leaning back with her arms stretched out in front of her. 'If you lean forward when she is going uphill and back when she is going downhill, it's a much nicer ride' Hugh called to Molly.

Molly leaned forward and felt instant relief. 'Well, that makes sense' Molly whispered to Red Rock, who was quietly following Firefly as their hooves drummed a rhythm on the land. As they reached the ridge, Hugh slowed Firefly down to a stop and the picture widened of the valley below. The forest covered one side of the valley and a river was flowing down the centre. The backdrop was a bright blue sky. Molly rode up and Red Rock stopped alongside Firefly.

'Oh wow, it's amazing!' Molly said in awe. Hugh leaned forward and rested his arms on the saddle horn. 'Ben brought me here, like his grandad brought him. It's a real special place, where everything is in perfect peace and harmony' Hugh said, as the view began to soothe his soul. Hugh swung his leg over, stepping off Firefly and sitting down on a nearby rock.

Molly clumsily got down too. As her feet hit the ground she lost her balance. She fell back and ended up flat on the floor, causing Red Rock to step back. Hugh began to chuckle. 'Hey, shush you' Molly said, getting up and dusting herself off as she moved across and sat on the rock next to Hugh.

They sat there in silence and watched the world drift on by. 'I have never felt so wonderful' Molly said, breaking the silence. 'Everything seems to make sense, like all the illusions just disappear' Molly said, looking across to Hugh. 'I know exactly what you mean' he replied, not taking his eyes off the landscape. They returned to silence as the sun continued to drift across the clear blue sky as time vanished into a single moment.

'We'd better be heading back' Hugh said, as he got up from the rock. 'Why so soon?' Molly disagreed. Hugh took out his phone. 'Molly, it's dinnertime' Hugh said, showing the clock on his phone. 'What? It can't be!' she squinted, as she read five o'clock on the screen. Hugh smiled. 'There is no time in nature, just a series of moments. Come on, I'll give you a leg up' he said. Molly slowly stood up, staring at Red Rock. 'And how am I supposed to get up there exactly?' she said, flummoxed.

'Come over here would you?' Hugh said, pointing at the stirrup. Molly reluctantly walked over and stood where Hugh had pointed. 'Put that hand there, and that hand here, right, on three pull yourself up. One, two…' Molly began to giggle as her knees went weak. 'Molly, quit giggling' Hugh said, frustrated, causing Molly to giggle even more. 'Oh, for goodness sake' Hugh suddenly grabbed Molly's legs and lifted her up. 'Pull yourself on' Hugh said breathlessly. Molly began to focus as she pulled her body into the saddle.

Hugh let go, bending over as he gasped for air. 'No more pancakes for you' he said jokingly as he lined Firefly up alongside the rock. As he stepped into the saddle, an owl swooped down between them. 'Wow, did you see that?' Molly said, pointing to the owl as it flew by them and down into the valley.

Hugh followed it with his eyes. 'That's strange, there was always one that used to sit in a tree outside Nana O's cottage' Molly said, as she turned Red Rock round and pointed her down the hill. 'You don't think it's another omen do you?' Hugh asked, as he walked Firefly on. 'Maybe. But what message is it trying to tell us?' Molly said as she rode, this time leaning back as they headed down the hill. 'I don't know but I know someone who will' Hugh said, asking Firefly to walk faster.

Ben walked across towards the gate as he spotted the two of them riding back. 'Did you have fun, kids?' he asked as he swung open the gate. 'What does the owl mean?' Hugh asked, as he stopped in front of him. 'The owl?' Ben asked curiously. 'Yeah, one flew right between us whilst we were getting back on the horses' Molly said, as Red Rock stopped with her head on Ben's chest. Ben reached up and stroked her head. 'Hello, you' he muttered to Red Rock.

'Well' Ben said, as he motioned for them to carry on through the gate. Hugh and Molly walked forward and then stopped again as Ben closed the gate behind them and stood in the middle. 'They say that the owl reminds us to see what others do not see, seeing beyond deceit and masks, an owl brings wisdom but with wisdom comes change, asking us to let go of a part of our lives to make room for something new' Ben said, looking at Hugh and then at Molly.

'But what has that got to do with us?' Molly asked, still bewildered. 'That I don't know, but it's shown up for a reason and I'm sure we won't have to wait long to find out the answer. OK, you two go and un-tack the horses and put them back in their stalls and come in. Dinner is nearly ready' Ben said, motioning for them to hurry.

Molly and Hugh asked Firefly and Red Rock to walk on as they headed back to the barn. Ben looked down at his boots and kicked the dust. 'Hhmm, the signposts are all pointing to one destination' Ben thought to himself, before walking back into the house. As he walked through the front door he was greeted by Ally in floods of tears, holding the phone in her hands.

Ally began waving the phone at Ben as no words would come out her mouth, tears continuing to stream down her cheeks. Ben urgently took the phone as he placed it to his ear. It was silent. 'Ally, there is no one there' Ben said frantically. Ally suddenly became motionless as she saw Hugh and Molly walking across to the house. As they stepped through the front door they immediately stopped next to Ben. 'Mom, what's wrong?' Hugh asked, alarmed.

Ally stepped across and sat down at the kitchen table. Ben, Molly and Hugh walked quickly across to join her, as Ben placed the phone down in front of him. Ally closed her eyes. 'Please give me strength she prayed' as she slowly opened her eyes and looked straight across the table at Ben, who was becoming more anxious.

'I have just had a phone call from England' Ally paused as she took another breath as the tears began to fall again. 'There has been an accident' Ally said, as she looked across to Molly. Molly continued to look confused. 'Molly, I'm so sorry' Ally stuttered. 'But your mum and dad were in a car accident on the way back from the airport and when the rescue team got there they had already returned back to the stars' Ally finished. Ben lifted off his hat and ran his hands across his face and through his hair.

Hugh remained speechless. 'These things don't happen' Molly said, shaking her head and refusing to believe what she had just heard. She stood up. 'No! No! It can't be true!' Molly said, staring sternly at Ally. Ally's hands flew to her mouth out of despair.

The noise of a truck echoed as it raced down the dirt road, screeching to a halt just outside the house. They listened as they heard the car door open and slam shut, footsteps frantically heading towards the front door. As the front door flung opened they turned round to see Billy standing in the doorway.

Billy surveyed the room and realised his worst fears were confirmed. He paced across to Molly and crouched down. Molly lowered herself back into the chair as Billy presented her with a letter. 'Molly, I received a letter today from your Nana O. She must have posted it before she died, inside was this card addressed to you, she must have known our paths would cross' Billy said as he tentatively handed the card to Molly.

Molly held it in her hand and stared at her name in

Nana O's writing on the envelope. She turned it over, opened it up and slid out a card with a picture of an owl on the front. Molly looked across at Hugh. As Molly opened up the card she began to read:

To My Dearest Molly,

I'm sure by now you have been on quite the adventure. If you have received this card it must mean you have found the next piece to the puzzle, the next life truth.

Well done!

With every truth discovered it means change is imminent. Do not fear this but see it as an opportunity to practise what you have learned, and use the pieces of the puzzle to rebuild a new picture of your life. You will always be safe whilst under the protective gaze of the stars and, remember, miracles do happen every single day. No matter what, we all still love you and send our love to you every day.

I know tonight you'll lay in your bed,

Many tears will be shed,

Pouring out your heart of broken dreams and moments that lay ahead,

Let my love give you hope,

To keep fighting and help you to cope,

With the moments when you feel you're alone,

But always know that the path will be clear for you to return back home.

The day will arrive when you do the impossible,

An enigma to those who watch what's possible.

As you no longer feel two worlds apart,

And you discover the key that unlocks your own heart.

Soon you will stand before us, a beacon of hope for us all to see,

Leading us with love, knowing what is meant to be.

I am never far away,

Holding you in my heart as I watch you pray,

Reminding you that dreams can become real as you begin to heal

Always know you will succeed, you have my guarantee.

Let these words bring you hope, my love bring you courage and always believe that the path will become clear when you look in the mirror, seeing, believing and becoming the person you dream you'd be each year.

Love always

Nana O

Molly looked around at everyone who were all drenched in anticipation. 'What does it say?' Hugh asked, no longer able to contain himself. Molly glanced down at the card and she looked up at Hugh, staring straight into his eyes. She felt the familiar feeling rise from deep inside as she spoke:

'Hope'

Can You Help Us Reach 50 reviews?

We would love to hear what you thought about the book.

1. Go to Amazon

2. Type 'Naomi Sharp' into the search box and press enter

3. Click on the book

4. Scroll down until you reach the star chart

5. Click the button and write a review

Every review received is a wonderful gift each day, thank you

With gratitude,

Naomi

8 ABOUT THE AUTHOR

www.naomisharpauthor.com

Naomi began making notes when she was 10 years old, always having a notebook ready to jot down the next profound thought or idea.

Naomi began to each day write things down in her notebook. But it wasn't until 6 years on that Naomi would write her first book Living Life With The Glass Half Full, where she would be able to share her story of changing life's adversity into lessons learned. No sooner had she finished that book she was onto her next, as she became inspired to write A Diary Of Dreams, her first fiction. Naomi describes the experience as 'downloading a story, like a movie was playing in front of me and I was writing down what was happening moment by moment'.

Naomi continues to write as her passion grows to inspire people to heal and find happiness and hope in their life. She feels storytelling is an incredible way to pass on wisdom and life's truths.

Naomi Sharp trained as an Occupational Therapist but became fascinated in how horses help people to heal not only physically but also mentally and emotionally. Her passion for understanding how we can help our bodies to heal and our dreams to become reality has brought some breathtaking experiences into her life, as well as the opportunity to meet some incredible people and places.

During the day Naomi also runs her therapy centre for individuals with a mental, physical or emotional disability to come and spend time with horses and celebrate what makes them unique.

9 OTHER BOOKS BY NAOMI SHARP

A Diary Of Dreams (Universal Series Book 1)

A journey to remembering dreams come true

Finding love and happiness by living your dreams following the death of a family member. Hugh watched his mom Ally's happiness dissolve away as her depression took hold as all she could see was a new absence in her life of a love that was no longer there. Hugh dreamed of his mom finding her happiness, falling in love and rediscovering the magic of life, and allowing love that once was to transform as they embark on a new chapter in life. Hugh decided to create a map of dreams as a vision board of all the thing he wanted to happen in his life. This resulted in an adventure that took him and Ally to meet the people they needed to meet, the places they needed to go and the dreams they desired to experience on the road to discovering how truly magical life is. This book helps inspire you to plan and dream the life you're desiring, empowering women and children to have the courage to follow their heart's desires, and enabling their ambitions in life to flourish. An incredible story of how family, dreams and love can help you achieve anything you want.

A Locket of Love (Universal Series Book 2)

A journey to remembering to follow our intuition.

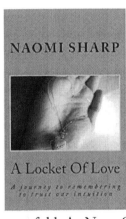

As Nana O waited for Molly to arrive she sat in her usual chair by the fire, as she twiddled her thumbs she began to think about the story that was going to be told about a locket and the secret it holds.

Molly arrived shuffling her feet not wanting to be there but as she sat down on the stool in front of Nana O she became captivated as the story began to unfold. As Nana O begins to tell the story about a single locket holding a secret that helps Molly to remember and understand how to follow her own intuition. Molly begins to follow it day by day as her life began to transform and she became the person she was meant to be. All the while being closely followed by her two best friends Layla and Dillon who are always there supporting her along the way. Throughout the book there are golden nuggets of wisdom that are there to help you to remember life truths that you may have forgotten. This is the second book in the universal series looking at the law of oneness, don't forget to check out the first book in this series A Diary of Dreams.

Living Life With The Glass Half Full

An inspiring true story of how a young girl chooses to learn from life's adversity with the help of horses. She travels to Ireland, France and America to understand how to live a better, happier life, and to understand what it truly means to heal. The story follows her from her younger days causing mischief in nursery through to the frustration of being dyslexic in school. This leads up to her whole world being turned around with a profound realisation. All the while different horses are guiding her path through the years with their constant friendship and companionship, highlighting some of the facts of life Naomi has picked up along the way. The book includes a bonus feature for your own personal development providing ways for you to analyse your life's problems and turn them into positives with surprising ease. It encourages you to work through your own challenges by changing your perceptions on how you view life and adversity so that you are able to change your life. This book provides a true account of how, by changing your own perceptions of life and looking for the lessons to be learned in the adversity, the adventure of life becomes more about using those lessons to help your dreams to become your reality rather than allowing the adversity to become your future.

40 Days Transforming Your Life

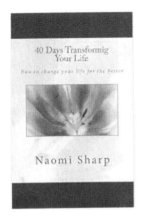

Are you ready for the journey of a lifetime, have you received enough of life's adversity that you are feeling your back is up against the wall?

Help has arrived!

In this how to book you will discover a *40 day process* that will help you and your life to transform, from a place of despair to the place where dreams come true.

You won't be doing this journey alone, every day you have a short chapter looking at what the day ahead has in store as you move up and down the emotional scale. In this 'how to' book it will explore what it means to change from the inside out and pearls of wisdom to keep you inspired and motivated to continue to move forward.

Aspects included in 40 Days Transforming Your Life

~ Letting go of past experiences
~ Loving yourself and your strengths
~ Learning to set a goal or dream

~ Setting up your routine for success
~ Celebrating your achievements
~ Worry no longer being a part of your day

40 Days Transforming Your Life book by Naomi Sharp helps you develop a simple but sustainable routine to reaching your goals, transforming your life, and living your dreams.

Printed in Great Britain
by Amazon